THE INVISIBLE WARRIOR

WINGS 3

THE
INVISIBLE WARRIOR

Charles Anthony

First published in Great Britain 1996
22 Books, Invicta House, Sir Thomas Longley Road,
Rochester, Kent

Copyright © 1996 by 22 Books

The moral right of the author has been asserted

A CIP catalogue record for this book is available from the
British Library

ISBN 1 898125 65 1

10 9 8 7 6 5 4 3 2 1

Typeset by Hewer Text Composition Services, Edinburgh
Printed in Great Britain by Cox and Wyman Limited, Reading

1

January 1941 was not a good month for the Tube. Bank Station got a direct hit one night, and 111 people died.

It was not a good month for Jack Shilling either. That same night as a brand-new, nineteen-year-old sergeant pilot, he was feeling the cold on the train that chugged its way northwards through the blacked-out Scottish countryside. It wasn't as if he was not dressed warmly. Next to his skin was his full-body underwear. Then his socks, shirt, tie and RAF blue serge trousers; then his RAF pullover, then the thick serge of his RAF best blue jacket. On top of all that was the blanket-like material of his greatcoat. And *still* he felt cold.

His dampened spirits, he reasoned, were not helping. He felt very much alone in this strange land. It had all been so different when he'd gone to volunteer for service in the Royal Air Force. Then, he'd been full of dreams of winging a Spitfire across the sky, charging valiantly at the enemy, dealing implacable death to those who had dared attack the mother country. He wished he had been in time for the Battle of Britain.

Instead, here he was on a cold train that seemed to be taking him to the ends of the earth. He'd long since lost count of the number of hours the laborious journey had so far taken. The training unit where he'd gained his wings seemed a lifetime away in Gloucestershire. He'd not got his dream: the Spitfire.

'You're going to Hurricanes,' the flight sergeant instructor at the initial training unit had told him. 'The CFI will give you the official gen.'

The Hurricane I at the advanced flying training school was no Spit but at least – even as the next best thing – it was a fighter, and he was a fighter pilot. He'd made it. They might have given him bombers. That did not bear thinking about.

But he was still paying a price. They were sending him into the middle of nowhere; out of sight. Making him invisible.

The chief flying instructor at the initial flying school, a squadron leader with a partly burned face who *had* been in the Battle, had said, 'I can see by your expression that you're disappointed, Shilling. Don't be. The Spitfire's got all the glory, but it's the Hurri that's got the tally of kills. Don't you forget that. Give me a choice and I'd take the Hurricane any day, without exception.'

He had tapped at his face. 'Got this in a Hurri, but I'm alive. In a Spit, I'd have been roasted.' He had grinned suddenly, strange little waves appearing on the polished skin of his right cheek. 'Spit. Roasted. Weak joke. I'd have bought the farm,' he'd gone on. 'The Hurri can take enormous punishment and at medium to low levels, she'll out-turn anything. You're a good pilot, Shilling. One of my best. Treat the Hurricane well, and she'll look after you. I want to hear great things about you wherever you go.'

'Yes, sir.'

'And don't bend any of His Majesty's precious fighters.'

'No, sir.'

'Or I'll come back to haunt you, even if the wretched Hun does manage to get me one day.'

'Yes, sir.'

Both the squadron leader and the flight sergeant – a veteran of the skies above Dunkirk – had been kind to him. He missed them.

At the advanced flying school, where he'd become friends with a Yorkshireman called Dan Silverdale, he had progressed well with the Hurricane. His determination to succeed had seen to that; but he still wished for a Spitfire.

'We're both foreigners down here,' Silverdale had

said with dry humour on their first meeting. 'We should stick together.'

But Silverdale had been washed out and had been sent on to the big but slow, locust-like Lysander. Quite a come-down, but he had taken the disappointment stoically. He would still be flying, after all. That was better than anything.

'So you'll be joining the Brylcreemed, top-button-undone heroes,' he'd commented ruefully as they'd said their goodbyes, 'while I go on to be a bus driver. Keep in touch with a poor mortal from time to time, won't you?'

'If I can find out where they send you, or you me.'

'I'll find a way.'

Not all the way up here, Shilling now thought gloomily. He missed Silverdale's warped sense of humour.

He stared out at the snowbound countryside, intermittently lit up by an eerie moon as it peeped through the clouds. The darkened carriage enabled him to see clearly, beyond the train. It was his first proper experience of winter and despite the surreal beauty of the landscape, he was not enjoying it.

This was so different from the warmth of Jamaica. The glorious autumn after the Battle had fooled him into believing the weather would always be mild. But a glorious autumn at the Gloucestershire operational training unit had not prepared him for such a sharp change. He doubted whether even those accustomed to British winters had been prepared for this cold. He'd seen many pinched faces, their owners looking very much the way he felt.

'Bit different from where you come from,' someone said to him in the gloom.

The speaker was a middle-aged Army sergeant who'd joined the train at Fort William with a group of soldiers who had filled the compartments and corridors. To Shilling, anyone above twenty was middle-aged. It was the first time the man had spoken, though he had stared at the stripes on Shilling's RAF greatcoat during the stop at Fort William. The entire train seemed full of military personnel.

'Yes,' Shilling agreed.

'Bit young to be a sergeant,' the Army man continued. 'Aircrew then, are you?'

'Yes,' Shilling repeated.

'Gunner?'

That was what the sergeant expected. The greatcoat hid the proud wings.

'Pilot,' Shilling corrected him as casually as he could.

He could sense the man's initial disbelief and knew, without looking, that other heads were turning his way.

'Army Co-operation?' the sergeant suggested, continuing the inquisition. If not a gunner, the voice seemed to be saying, then surely nothing more exalted than stooging around in utility aircraft like Ansons and suchlike.

'Fighters,' Shilling corrected him again, feeling a great deal of satisfaction as he did so. Fighters were an unattainable goal to many. It made up in some measure for being sent to the back of beyond.

Total silence greeted this revelation.

'Well, I never,' someone else said at last.

The sergeant was still silent.

'You're that good?' The sergeant had decided to get back into the conversation.

'Somebody must have thought so,' Shilling replied with diplomatic modesty.

'Show us your wings, then,' another voice demanded out of the dark. 'Here. I've got a small torch . . .'

'The blackout!' the sergeant snapped.

'It's only a wee thing, Sarge. I'll hide it with my hands. Just want a quick look, that's all. See if he's really got wings, or if he's shooting us a line. Wouldn't like that, would we?'

The sergeant's own curiosity got the better of him. 'All right,' he agreed eventually. 'But only a quick look, mind. Don't want some jumped-up young officer poking his head round the corner. Come on. Be quick about it.'

A weak light came on, cupped by the doubter's hands. 'Let's see those wings,' the disembodied voice insisted.

With an air of quiet resignation Shilling opened his greatcoat. The torch played its light above his left breast pocket.

'Well, it's true all right,' the voice said. 'He's got his wings. All shiny and new, though. No medal ribbons. A sprog. Top button's undone, so maybe he's really a fighter pilot. Still a sprog, all the same.'

'Now we've all had a look, douse that light,' the sergeant ordered.

'Never been in a fight, then?' he went on to Shilling.

'Not yet.'

'We've been in a few . . .' the man with the torch began.

'Careless talk, Jenkins!' the sergeant interrupted sharply.

'Sorry, Sarge.'

'And where're you off to?' the sergeant added to Shilling.

'Careless talk, Sergeant . . . as you've just said.' The length of the sentence made his Jamaican lilt more noticeable.

He could sense the other man staring hard at him in the ensuing silence.

'Fair enough,' the sergeant said at last.

The train clattered its way northwards.

When the train next came to a halt, it was the end of the line. By now it was daylight.

'All change!' Shilling heard coming faintly from outside. The announcement gradually grew louder as the speaker approached. 'All change! This train stops here! All change . . .' The stationmaster's voice moved on.

'All right, you dozy lot!' the sergeant barked. 'Get moving!'

There was the scuffling of booted feet as the soldiers began to make themselves ready.

Shilling felt uneasy. This was still a long way from where he was supposed to be going. If the train went no further, he'd have to scrounge a lift with the soldiers.

But the sergeant was saying, 'Our stop.' He held out a hand. 'Take it easy, mate. Get some Jerries for us, but don't let them get you.'

Shilling shook the hand. 'I'll do my best.'

'Same here, Sarge,' the doubting Thomas with the torch added, holding out a hand as well.

Shilling shook it. By the time the soldiers had filed off, he'd shaken at least ten hands. He watched as they stomped off the train. Soon the sergeant had them smartly lined up on the small platform, before setting them off at a brisk marching pace.

The engine blew clouds of steam which billowed in the cold air before tumbling about in the path of the soldiers. They marched into it until it hid them completely from view.

In the daylight, their faces had not seemed much older than his; but theirs had taken on the cold mien of veterans. Men who had already seen too much in their young lives. As the steam swallowed them, he wondered where they were going.

He climbed off the train, kitbag over his shoulder. The marching steps had long faded. As he turned to get his bearings, an unexpected sight greeted him. At a far end of the platform was a small group of men. Black men.

He was astonished to see them. They looked like civilians, but all wore thick winter work clothes that gave the semblance of uniforms. Despite the warm clothing, they looked grey and cold. They were staring at him as if at a rare creature in a zoo.

He sauntered towards them as they continued to stare silently. When he reached the group, he put down the kitbag. Some of them stared at it, reading his name.

'Where you from?' one finally asked. He sounded

Trinidadian. 'You really a sergeant? You look too young, boy.'

Shilling wanted to sigh. Now even the blacks didn't want to believe it.

'I've come up from the south,' he replied, 'and yes, I really am a sergeant.'

'He don't mean where the train come from, man,' another said. Jamaican.

'Jamaica.'

The Jamaican, a big man with still eyes, said, 'You talk like a white hofficer.' It sounded like an accusation.

'It's . . .' Shilling paused as a multiple roar broke into the conversation and made the men all look up urgently, poised to duck for shelter.

Shilling looked up, but made no move to run. He'd know the sound of Merlin engines anywhere. Four Hurricanes, in two pairs, swept low above the little station. The sight of them lifted his spirits. As he looked eagerly after them, he wondered whether they were from the squadron he was on his way to join.

The men, having recognized the RAF roundels, had once more turned their collective attention upon him.

'No use looking at them aeroplanes like that, boy,' the Trinidadian began. 'Only fancy white boys fly *them*.'

'So where you learn to talk like a hofficer?' the big Jamaican demanded, returning to his theme.

'I didn't learn anywhere, unless you count my school back home. This is how I talk. And at flying school,' Shilling went on defensively, 'there's a certain way of speaking that . . . grows on you . . .'

'*Flying* school? You dreaming, boy?' someone else put in.

They all stared at him as if he'd lied to them.

'They make *you* a *pilot*?' another said, the scepticism so palpable it was as if the speaker had found the idea totally outrageous.

This time, Shilling did sigh. Might as well get it over with, he reasoned. They'd be asking soon enough.

'Would you like to see my wings?'

'Yeah, man. We would. This we got to see.' They clearly still did not believe him.

How ironic, he thought. Doubted by both sides. He opened the greatcoat.

'Shit,' one said. 'It damn true!'

The big Jamaican grinned. 'A *Jamaican* pilot. None of that small-island rubbish.'

'Shut your damn mouth, Price,' a new voice, clearly a small-islander, snapped. 'He be a *pilot*, and one of us. Be proud for *all* of us. What kind of pilot?' he added to Shilling, who had re-buttoned his greatcoat.

11

Shilling pointed in the direction the Hurricanes had taken. 'Fighter.'

They all whistled, impressed.

'Hot damn!' the Trinidadian said, suddenly friendly and basking in reflected glory. 'Hot damn! Good for you, boy. Good for you.'

'Hard for whites to make fighter pilot,' the big Jamaican began. 'How come you make it? You know somebody with power?'

Shilling shook his head. 'No.'

It was not strictly true. He did know someone, but not with any real power. The person in question, however, had helped him get this far. His former schoolmaster.

'And what are you all doing here?' he now asked them, the Jamaican lilt unconsciously more pronounced. 'I didn't expect to see another black face in this place.'

The Trinidadian made a sucking noise of disgust. 'We come to fight for the mother country. Volunteers, you know. So what these people do?' he continued. 'They send us to freeze our balls up here, to cut wood! Cut wood, man! Such stupidness!'

'"And they shall be hewers of wood",' someone Shilling could not see intoned biblically.

'And fetch and carry,' another added. 'We here to pick up cargo from this train.'

'They scared to give us weapons, perhaps,' the big

12

Jamaican said with a grin full of irony. 'They think we shoot them and rape their women. They think we jungle animals. But they give you the biggest weapon of all, man. They must like you.'

'I . . .' Shilling began, but an imperious voice interrupted him.

'You there!' came the shout from behind him along the platform. 'Are you the driver?'

'Shit,' the Trinidadian said. 'Here come ol' Horse-arse.'

'Who?' Shilling had turned towards the sound of the voice.

A figure in Army uniform was approaching purposefully.

'The man in charge,' the Trinidadian replied contemptuously. '*Leftenant* Grigg. Look at his face. A *real* horse-arse.'

Lieutenant James Algernon Grigg had been a bright young officer during the First World War, the toast of his peers for his daring, both in battle and with the ladies. Jags Grigg everyone had called him then. He'd finished the war as a much-decorated major; but he'd no longer been the same Jags Grigg. The years of slaughter in the trenches had, as they had done to so many of his friends who had managed to survive, destroyed the bright young man. In his place had come a drink-ridden cynic.

13

After the war he'd wound up in various posts in the colonies, had seen the future stretching interminably ahead, and had sought further solace in the bottle. It had almost been a relief to be welcomed with open arms, the madness of Hitler that had once more brought war upon the world. He would get back into proper uniform. The sound of gunfire would be his salvation.

But it had not worked out like that. The bastards at the War Office had taken one look at him, he fumed incessantly, and had chosen to ignore his outstanding war record. He had not expected to be reinstated as a major. He'd expected a drop in rank, certainly to captain. And even if they'd decided not to send him immediately into battle, he could have marked time in some Intelligence post. His knowledge was extensive and useful, the drink notwithstanding.

But what they'd done to him could not have been a worse slap in the face. They had made him a *second* lieutenant, in the *Home Guard*, and had given him a bunch of wood-cutting blacks to look after. Some of his old friends would soon be colonels. He didn't see them any more. He could not face their pity.

With these bitter thoughts churning through his mind, Grigg advanced on the unknown, uniformed black man.

Now they were sending him more blacks. Where did they think he was? Back in the colonies?

'Are you the driver?' he repeated crossly.

Shilling looked calmly back at the irate Home Guard officer.

'No,' he replied.

The men stared at him transfixed, amazed by the tone he'd used. It had not been impolite, but neither had it been deferential.

'No, *sir*!' Grigg snarled. 'You are in uniform and even though I may seem to be just a Home Guard officer to you, I am still an officer and you *will* address me properly and salute me! What uniform is that?'

'Royal Air Force . . . sir,' Shilling replied, his voice indicating plainly that Grigg ought to have known his uniforms by now. He gave an awkward salute.

Grigg snapped one back and bristled at the imagined insubordination. 'You'll have to change your attitude, my lad, if you're going to get on with me. Name?'

'Sergeant Shilling . . . sir. And I am not your driver. I have not been posted to you.'

'Not posted . . . then what are you doing here?'

'I'm on my way to my unit . . . sir.'

'And where is that?'

'I do not have the authority to tell you . . . sir.'

Grigg's drink-sodden eyes glared at him. 'Are you toying with me, Sergeant?'

'No . . . sir. It's just that I am not authorized to tell you the location of my unit. I would be breaking Air Force regulations.'

Grigg did not have an answer to that. It only served to make him more furious. To make things worse, the men appeared to be enjoying the exchange.

At that moment a newcomer, in RAF blue, came on to the platform. He was an aircraftman, much older than Shilling. He glanced at the men and Shilling without interest, before looking at Grigg.

'I'm here to pick up a pilot. Seen him?'

Grigg turned his fire upon the RAF man. 'Doesn't the Royal Air Force teach its personnel to show the proper respect to officers?' he roared. '*What is your name?*'

The airman was taken aback by the storm-force bellow. He frowned uncertainly, and peered at the Home Guard shoulder patch. His expression clearly said Home Guard officers were not really officers as such. 'Creddon . . . sir.' It was almost exactly as Shilling had done.

'Well, Creddon, do I look as if I'm holding your pilot? Do you see any pilots around here?'

Clearly expecting what he would have termed a proper officer, Creddon ignored Shilling. 'No . . . sir.'

'Then go and look for him! Don't tell me you RAF types lose your pilots before they've even been in battle!'

'Yes, sir . . . and no . . . sir.' Creddon hurried away before Shilling could say anything.

The men were studying Shilling. Their various expressions seemed to be a mix of renewed doubt as to his real status, and anticipation. They wanted to see Grigg's expression when Shilling revealed his true identity.

Creddon soon returned. 'He's not here,' he said to Grigg. He looked confused.

'Then clearly he's missed the train.' Grigg made it sound as if it was the fault of the entire Royal Air Force, and Creddon's in particular.

'I'm your pilot,' Shilling said.

Creddon managed to look both startled and confused at the same time. Grigg's red eyes widened in disbelief. The men's expressions had now changed into a collective smirk.

'*You?*' Creddon began, then, as if seeing the stripes for the first time: 'Er . . . Sarge?' Confusion and disbelief chased across his stoat-like features.

'Me,' Shilling assured him.

'Well, bugger me,' Creddon remarked softly.

Grigg seemed ready to explode. 'Why the devil didn't you say?' he demanded savagely, glaring at Shilling. 'You *were* trying to make a fool of me!'

'I was not . . . sir. You never gave me a chance to tell you.'

'Are you now questioning what *I* say, Sergeant?'

'No . . . sir.'

Grigg stared biliously at each of the RAF men. 'Get out of here! Both of you!'

Creddon needed no second bidding and almost sprinted away.

Shilling grabbed his kitbag. 'Good luck,' he said to the men.

'Take care of yourself up there, boy,' the Jamaican said.

'I'll do my best.'

'And get one for us.'

'I'll do that too.'

First the soldiers, now these men from the islands. He hoped he could keep all these promises.

'That's enough!' Grigg snapped. 'This is not a social gathering. All right, you men. Get to work! We haven't got all day!'

Shilling looked at him. 'We are on the same side . . . sir. Aren't we?'

He walked away before the Home Guard officer could make any comment. He sensed Grigg's angry eyes boring into his back until he left the platform.

*   *   *

Creddon was waiting behind the wheel of the small saloon that had been sent for the pick-up. Shilling couldn't understand it. The squadron commander must definitely have been expecting an officer. Small utility lorries were what sergeants rated, even though strictly speaking, it was cheaper to send a small car. Less use of valuable petrol for a start. Perhaps the squadron commander did know and was being practical.

Creddon's next words soon killed that idea as Shilling put his kit behind the front seats and climbed in. The engine was already running, but the car was barely warmer inside.

'The squadron CO will have a fit.'

'What do you mean?'

'Are you really a pilot?'

For reply, Shilling wearily went into the routine and opened the greatcoat briefly.

'Better you than me, Sarge,' Creddon said as he crunched into first gear. The car jerked itself away from the station.

'That doesn't sound as if I'm going to get a warm welcome,' Shilling said.

Creddon glanced at him. 'Do you know about the CO?'

'I know his name. Squadron Leader Paul du Toit. Free French?'

'If only.'

'I don't understand.'

'You will, Sarge,' Creddon said ominously as the car nosed its way cautiously along the narrow, twisting road. 'You will.'

Shilling looked out at the frozen landscape. 'How far are we from the squadron?'

'Give or take a few miles, nearly ninety . . .'

'*Ninety?* Isn't there a railway station closer?'

''Fraid not. We're really marooned up there. A lot of the officers usually fly their aircraft up. Didn't they have one for you?'

'I feel as if I've been on a train for years. I didn't know I could fly up. No one said.'

'Probably because we've got the new Hurricane IIs.'

'Perhaps. I've never flown one. I'm qualified on the Hurricane I, though.'

'You'll soon get the hang of it.' Creddon darted another glance at Shilling.

'Why do you keep looking at me like that?'

Creddon cleared his throat noisily as the car whined its way round a steep bend. 'We . . . er don't get er . . . many of you up our way, Sarge, if you don't mind my saying so.'

'I don't mind,' Shilling said with resignation, knowing precisely what the driver meant.

'It's just that . . .' Creddon paused.

'It's just what?' Shilling asked.

But Creddon had decided not to say more. 'I'd

better not be talking out of turn.' He closed the subject.

Ninety miles of this, Shilling thought gloomily.

'Done any night flying?'

Shilling woke with a start, and soon wished he hadn't. He'd been dozing, trying to forget the cold that was apparently determined to freeze his feet off. He'd been wishing he'd worn his flying boots; but he soon forgot about frozen extremities.

The car was slithering its way down what seemed to be a precipitous slope. There was a bend at the bottom that wound its way out of sight. They'd never make it.

He glanced anxiously at Creddon. Wouldn't it be ironic, he thought, if he died on this mountain road before he'd even gone into battle?

But Creddon seemed perfectly at ease. The car continued to slither under the driver's control and negotiated the bend without drama.

'Don't worry, Sarge,' Creddon said. 'I've been on this road so many times I know it like the back of my hand.'

'Picked up a lot of people, have you?'

'I'm the one that gets sent.'

And how many survived? he wanted to ask.

'Well, Sarge?' Creddon was saying, then after a

slight pause, he repeated his earlier question: 'Done any night flying?'

'I've got some hours.'

'You'll need them all.' Creddon peered briefly upwards through the small windscreen. There was no sunlight to speak of. 'As you can see, even during the day it's like a sort of twilight this far north, at this time of year. Good weather today. We can see where we're going.'

'How bad does it get?' Shilling asked, certain he was not going to like the reply.

'Pretty bad sometimes. We've had winds that have turned the aeroplanes over and even ripped the roofs off a couple of buildings.'

Shilling let Creddon's words sink in. And *this* is where they've sent me?

Only the thought of flying the Hurricane kept his spirits up. That, at least, was something to look forward to, even in this bleak landscape.

He was eager to fly. As far as he was concerned, every minute spent on the ground was wasted. He could barely wait to see the new aircraft, one of which was going to be *his*. It was a thought worth savouring.

Creddon was glancing at Shilling again, only partially reading the other man's expression correctly.

'It won't be so bad,' he said, thinking how young the pilot looked. 'At least, we've got good food.

Better than a lot of other RAF stations. We've got a joke. Even other ranks eat better than officers at some of the other stations.'

Shilling smiled weakly.

Creddon wondered how long this one would last. Of the twelve or so pilots he'd picked up since being posted to the station, eight had died. Most had gone into the drink during a storm. Lost and short of fuel.

He felt sorry for Shilling. It didn't help much, having a CO like du Toit.

Until the war, the only black men Creddon had seen had been in the newsreels and the pictures. Those in the pictures mostly went about half-naked and tended to look on whites as supper. Those in the newsreels were in items about the colonies. Even when war had come, except for those poor bastards he sometimes saw at the railway station, he'd never actually met one, although he knew some were joining the services.

He glanced at Shilling once more. This one looked so bloody young. Probably scared too. He ought to be, especially of the CO. Creddon was astonished by the amount of sympathy he felt for the black pilot.

Poor bloody blighter, he thought.

His Hilda would never have believed it. She hated black people and actually believed they all swung in trees like Tarzan, talking in their mumbo-jumbo language. That was the pictures for you. That was Hilda for you. She believed everything she saw on that screen.

He gave Shilling another surreptitious glance. What would Hilda make of *him*? A *black* sergeant who was also a Hurricane pilot.

'You mean *he* can give you orders?' she would probably say, eyes wide with horror at the thought of it.

He'd have to say yes and she'd have a fit thinking about it.

It could have been worse. They could have made him an officer. Now that would have been something.

2

While Shilling was trying to keep his feet warm on the back roads of northern Scotland, Dan Silverdale was fervently wishing that things were a lot less hot, metaphorically speaking, where he was.

Now a flight sergeant, he had rapidly built a reputation for daring airmanship at the special unit to which he had been assigned. Already a veteran with ten missions under his belt, he was the proud holder of the Distinguished Flying Medal.

He'd been given the gong for successfully out-flying two Messerschmitt Me-109s that had been determined to shoot him down over the fields of France one early morning. Their failure had enabled him to bring an important agent safely back to England.

It had been the agent's testimony, describing Silverdale's astonishing low-flying prowess among the trees and sometimes so close to the ground that it frequently looked like an attempt at a high-speed landing, that had put the seal on the recommendation for the medal. One of the 109s had slammed into the trees during the frustrated effort to bring him down. So, despite not being a fighter pilot as he'd dreamed, Silverdale had got his first kill. The swastika denoting his vanquished enemy now adorned the Lysander III, beneath its cockpit rim.

But he was not thinking of victories as he waited anxiously on the edge of a secluded field, once again in France. There was far too much light around for comfort. Normally he would have been out of this place long ago, heading home under the cover of darkness. Unit standing orders were, if the parties didn't show by a specific time – which included an added margin to allow for unavoidable changes in the original plan – take-off was to be implemented, no matter who was going to be left behind.

Normally.

But this was not normal. His orders were to wait until the last possible moment. A package was to be brought to him. Its importance was such that even the risk of being caught or shot down had been considered acceptable. The mission planners had assured him this did not mean he was expendable.

'You could have fooled me,' he now muttered, tensely peering about him, hoping to see friendly figures hurrying towards the aircraft. What was one flight sergeant more or less? The package was the thing.

But the woods were silent. Nothing moved. It was as if no one else in the world existed. There were no sounds of transport vehicles on the road he'd flown over, just under a mile away; no sounds of the ubiquitous motorcycle combinations of roving German patrols. There was not even the distant sound of warfare to introduce a dose of reality. The Lysander, its engine silent so as not to betray its presence to any passing troops, waited like a huge insect, as if pausing for breath.

The longer the wait, the less Silverdale liked it. His margin had long since disappeared. Any moment now a patrol would put in an appearance. It was inevitable. The hope was that he'd be away before that happened.

He scanned the lightening sky anxiously, and hoped any prowling Messerschmitts would not decide to come close enough to spot him.

Without the engine to supply heating, it had now become cold within the cockpit, but Silverdale still felt warm in his cold-weather flying clothing. In fact, he felt hot; but it had nothing to do with the ambient temperature. Sitting exposed like this, in the middle of Occupied France, should chill the blood; but perversely, he felt as if someone had stuck him in a furnace.

As he sat there waiting, he allowed his mind to take him back to the time he'd been ploughed out of the fighter-pilot stream and sent to one of the special-duties units in Norfolk. There'd been an unexpected and exotic mix of aircraft at the unit: bombers, utilities, reconnaissance types and others whose eventual applications he could only guess at. He'd stared at them, his mind full of questions he knew would not be answered. It was not the kind of place to ask questions about matters that did not directly concern you.

His heart had leapt when he'd seen both Spitfires and Hurricanes among the assembled aeroplanes. Perhaps he *would* get fighters, after all. There were some people – mainly those who had failed to get their first choice of aircraft – who believed that there were sadistic selectors hidden somewhere within the depths of the Service whose greatest delight in life was the hammering of square pegs into round holes. The harder it was to force the peg to fit, the better these mythical sadists seemed to like it. Silverdale had begun to consider that a fact of life – until he saw those Spits and Hurris. But the dream was a forlorn one.

What he'd got was the Lysander.

At first, looking at the Lizzie – as just about every-body called it – with its locust body slung beneath its strutted high wing, he'd felt a great despair. Its stubby, fixed main undercarriage, be-spatted with wheels encased in substantial fairings, made him feel as if he should be studying entomology instead of learning to fly the thing. True, he'd still be flying; but . . .

Then the aircraft had begun to get to him; and while Jack Shilling had been getting to grips with the power of the Hurricane I, Silverdale had been coming to terms with the idiosyncrasies of his new aircraft. Soon he had begun to enjoy flying it. After becoming operational and experiencing his first mission, he realized that he'd been picked for talents he'd never known he'd possessed. The peg hammerers, after the usual quota of abortive tries, had actually found a round peg for a round hole.

The Lysander, he'd subsequently discovered, had lots of tricks in its armoury, and in some versions a sting in the tail too. One of its sister aircraft had actually shot down the first bomber – a Heinkel III – to be destroyed over friendly forces, back in November '39.

Those funny-looking fairings on the wheels each housed a .303-calibre Browning gun, with 500 rounds apiece. Additionally, there were two 20mm Hispano cannon, one fixed on each side of the undercarriage. Some variants – but not his – carried another twin Browning in the rear cockpit. In those early days of the war Lysanders had, incredibly, done their time as night-fighters and had also carried out some ferocious ground attacks against enemy columns.

The Westland Lysander was a versatile, multi-role aircraft. It had a fantastic short-field take-off and landing capability. It could carry bombs on its earth-skimming missions and, with its standard fit of cameras, perform photo-recce tasks. It was frequently used as an armament practice aircraft.

Silverdale considered he had the best version. There were no Brownings in the tail and therefore no gunner. He had his two cannon and two Browning forward guns, his recce cameras, his automatic gun camera. There were the automatic inboard and outboard slats on the wing leading edge. These ran the entire length of the wing, with inboard and outboard operating independently of each other.

The inboard slats and the flaps operated in concert. The entire system was deployed fully automatically, depending on the speed of the aircraft. The Lysander was remarkably agile in its own environment and Silverdale exploited this quality to the full. It had helped him confound the Me-109s.

There was solid armour plating behind him and

at his sides; in the rear cockpit too. Most of the Lizzies that did the pick-up jobs had more passenger space, and were therefore somewhat heavier and slower, in some cases *under* 200mph max. But his had just room for one in the rear, carried less weighty equipment and thus, much lighter and with a slightly more powerful engine, could do a respectable 260mph in level flight, and pass 300 in the dive. Which was a lot better than the 138mph biplaned Swordfish that some Navy types had to fly, and not all that far from the maximum 318mph level-flight speed of the early Hurricane Is.

All in all, he thought as he looked about him, he hadn't done too badly. His unit was less formal than those on more orthodox RAF stations. He had a fair degree of autonomy and promotion seemed to come reasonably quickly. A friendly, non-flying warrant officer on the administrative staff had hinted to him that it wouldn't be long before he was advanced to warrant rank – or even recommended for a commission if he kept up the good work.

If I don't die out here first, he now thought grimly. Bye, Flight Sergeant Silverdale.

Or very much worse as far as he was concerned: end up wounded and captured. The enemy was not known to be kind to those involved in clandestine operations.

He could imagine what some Gestapo man would say to him.

Flight Sergeant Silverdale, for you the war is over. You will be shot!

As he contemplated the grim possibility, he idly wondered how 'Bob' Shilling was getting on, and whether he'd as yet scored a kill.

Then all thoughts of Shilling vanished from his mind. He'd detected movement at the far edge of the woods. Friendly? Enemy?

Then, distinctly, he heard the sound of gunfire.

Swiftly, he began to go through the start-up procedures. There were no fewer than seventeen separate actions to take to complete the process. Although the engine had been switched off, it was still warm, so priming time could be halved. His hands seemed to move around the cockpit in a blur.

Throttle – half-inch open; mixture control – normal; airscrew pitch control – pulled out for coarse pitch; fuel cock – on; gills – opened fully; carburettor heat intake – control pushed in for cold; carburettor priming cock – prime by unscrewing and operating pump until sudden pressure felt; turn priming cock to 'prime engine'; engine still warm, so four strokes instead of eight; with ignition switches off, turn engine by starter until priming complete; close priming cock, screw down priming pump;

main ignition switches on; press starter button – to hell with the noise, it was go or stay here for ever – engine firing OK, so switch off starting magneto; engine ticking over, so watch oil inlet temperature; pull out carburettor heat intake slightly to let in some warm air to compensate for the cold-weather start; now push in heat intake to admit cold air; push in oil heat control knob; ease throttle forward slightly. Wait.

Someone was running across the frost-covered, hard-packed open ground. The tall, frost-draped trees were like brittle, motionless sentinels, surrounding the clearing. Beyond them, a thin blanket of snow formed a diaphanous white shroud for the woods.

Silverdale watched the running figure – in a long, belted field coat – who carried what looked like a briefcase in one hand. The other held a Sten sub-machine-gun. As the runner got closer, he saw it was a young woman. The beret that had concealed her hair had fallen, causing her long, dark tresses to bounce about her shoulders as she ran.

Any firing would have been drowned out inside the cockpit by the sound of the engine; but he could see no one following, or shooting at her. Then he saw more figures appear at the edge of the wood. They wore civilian clothes. Several dropped to the ground to face the way they had come and began firing back into the woods.

Resistance fighters.

He understood what they were doing. They were giving the running woman cover.

He also realized why they were late. They must have been fighting a rearguard action all the way here. He wondered how many German troops were now involved in the chase. It was certainly going to be a hairy take-off.

The young woman had reached the left side of the aircraft. He slid a side window open. The sounds of firing were clear now. A mortar shell landed among a small group of the Resistance fighters. Bodies flew through the air and those still in one piece lay unmoving where they had fallen.

Soon, Silverdale thought, the mortars would be targeting the aircraft.

'Go around to the right!' he yelled at the young woman. 'There's a hand-grip low down on the side of the aircraft. Pull that! It's a ladder. Climb up, slide the canopy and get into the back!'

'I am not coming!' she shouted in perfectly good, French-accented English. 'This is for you!'

Coming close to the left side of the aircraft, she slung the Sten across her back to free her hand, gripped the rear wing strut to steady herself against the propwash as it blew her long hair backwards and, with some difficulty, raised the briefcase towards the side of the cockpit. It looked heavy.

'Now she tells me,' he muttered to himself.

He released his straps and leaned across to reach down and grab the briefcase, which he hauled in.

'Thank you!' she called at him. 'Now I must go and help my friends! Go! *Allez!*'

Without waiting for his comment she ran back towards where her compatriots were fighting for their lives. She even paused long enough to retrieve her beret before dashing on. He had a vivid memory of bright eyes as he watched the hurrying figure.

My God, he thought. She's running straight to her death.

He hoped the bloody briefcase was worth it.

No time to worry about her. He had to get off before things got even hotter. He shut the side window, secured his straps and opened the throttle wide. The Lysander began to move at last.

But it was not to be.

Something ominous swooped down and hurtled towards him, spitting flame. He squeezed at the brake lever at the base of the hollow of the control column spade grip. The Lysander came to a rude halt. The hard ground of the clearing was erupting into gouts of frosted earth. The troops in the woods had called out the cavalry. The Me-109s had arrived.

There were two of them. Both missed because their pilots, scared of slamming into the trees, had pulled up sharply to avoid the clutching branches. This gave Silverdale a breathing space to work out his tactics.

What tactics? he thought as he looked about him, hoping for an idea. His options were limited, to say the least.

Then he remembered something he'd noted as daylight approached and decided it was the only choice he had, *if* he could make it work. His only other option was to abandon the aircraft. This he had no intention of doing. He was not going to scrub the mission, nor had he any desire to walk his way out of France.

He reduced engine rpm to a tick-over. At the far edge of the clearing people began to turn round questioningly as they heard the change of cadence in the engine. Within the front of the wheel housings were each of the Lysander's two landing lights. Silverdale now switched them on and off twice. To make the point he cut the engine, once more uncoupled his harness, opened the cockpit and climbed out.

He could imagine their consternation. But it was the only way to concentrate their minds quickly.

He flung himself flat on the ground as a screaming double roar warned of the approach of the 109s

for a second pass. Again the combined machine-gun and cannon fire of the Messerschmitts tore at the hard ground. Again the proximity of the trees to their flight path forced them to pull up early, and again they missed.

But it wouldn't and couldn't last. Sooner or later one of the pilots would be brave enough to come lower or, frustrated, call the target for the mortars. Goodbye, Lysander. Hello, long walk home.

As the Messerschmitts rose angrily for a third pass, Silverdale could see people running along the edge of the clearing towards him. There were four this time. The young woman accompanied them.

He got to his feet as they approached.

The young woman rushed up, breathing hard, her bright eyes blazing at him. 'What are you doing?' she demanded angrily. 'We are holding back the Boche for you to take off. My people have risked . . .'

'If I try to take off,' he interrupted, cutting through her anger, 'those 109s will cut me down before I've got flying speed. Then your precious briefcase won't be going anywhere, will it? And before you explode with anger, ask your friends to help me move the aircraft . . .' He glanced at the three burly, stony-faced men who had come with her. They looked more like bodyguards, and twice as mean.

'You are *moving* the aeroplane? You are crazy!'

'Perhaps, but if you want your package to get to London, I suggest you help me.'

'If you cannot take off, leave the plane! We will burn it to prevent the Boche from getting their hands on it. We will find some other way to get the package to London.'

'I'm not leaving my aircraft here,' Silverdale told her calmly. 'The more you stand arguing with me, the less are our chances of making it out of here alive.'

As if to confirm his words, the Messerschmitts were back. All five hit the ground as bullets and cannon shells raked the area for a third time, to the background roar of engines at full power. It was third time still lucky. No one was hurt and the Lizzie was still intact.

'They're going to come up with a new idea soon,' Silverdale told the young woman from where he lay. 'They won't miss for ever.'

She had dropped to the ground close to him and their faces were turned towards each other. Down there in the relative gloom, her eyes seemed dark.

Beyond them, the sounds of the ferocious exchange of fire within the woodland continued unabated.

He stood up once more and saw that the men were staring hard at him.

'It's all right,' he told them drily. 'I didn't touch her.'

The young woman sprang to her feet. 'You are making jokes?'

'Trying to liven up the proceedings,' he told her straight-faced. 'If you look just a little way behind the aircraft, you'll see a slight depression. I want to push it backwards in there, and I'll need help to push it out again when this is over.'

She looked puzzled. 'What are you trying to do?'

'Trying is right,' he remarked grimly. 'Come on. Help me. Two at the front on each wing strut and one to guide the tail. You take the tail.' Without waiting to hear what she had to say to that, he went to a wing strut and held on to it, then looked at the others expectantly.

She hesitated briefly then spoke to the men in French, adding something else for good measure which made them chuckle.

Probably told them I'm crazy, Silverdale thought.

But that didn't matter, because they were now helping him to manoeuvre the Lizzie.

Cautiously but with speed, they eased the aircraft back into the depression, leaving the main wheels on its rim. The Lysander now had a pronounced nose-up stance.

Silverdale stood briefly to one side to study the posture. It just might work.

'What are you doing now, you crazy man?' the young woman asked in a voice that demanded a reply. But she no longer displayed the dismissive arrogance of the Resistance fighter towards someone whom she clearly considered to be little more than a messenger boy, and with whom she was forced to give full co-operation.

Silverdale pointed. 'Look at those guns on the wheels. Follow the lines of the barrels and see where they're aiming.'

After looking from the weapons to a point in the sky and back again, the young woman smiled at him. That smile was a transformation. The prematurely hardened face had softened into something of heart-stopping beauty. Beneath the warrior pose was someone quite soft, trying very hard to remain hidden. He could fully understand why the men were so protective of her.

'You are crazy,' she insisted. 'But perhaps it will work.'

'I hope so,' he said fervently. 'We'll have just the one chance. When those guns fire they'll get the hint very quickly and call up even more cavalry. If we get one, it should buy just about enough time for me to get off.' Then he said something rash. 'If we do get out of this,' he continued, glancing at

the Sten she carried, 'I've got a little present you might like.'

Leaving the young woman to stare uncomprehendingly at him, Silverdale climbed quickly back into the Lysander's cockpit.

'Must have been that smile,' he muttered to himself as he started the engine once more and left it at tick-over.

Attached to the top left of the spade grip of the control stick was a vertical three-way switch that controlled the guns. They could be fired independently or together. He decided to go for the whole works and selected both guns and cannon. In addition to the reflector gun-sight, the Lysander also had an alternative bead and ring set-up, just like the old First World War fighters. The bead was attached to the top of the engine cowling while the ring was positioned on the windscreen.

'All right,' he said to the angry, prowling Messerschmitts. 'I'm ready for you.'

Oberleutnant Helmut Loring was leader of the two 109Es. He was frustrated, and was seething as he prepared for the fourth pass.

'This time,' he began sharply to his number two, Leutnant Karl Zürst, 'we get that Tommy. It was a wretched aircraft like this one that caused Hansi to hit the trees.'

If Zürst thought it would be more prudent to call up some mortar fire and roast the woods instead of trying to commit suicide against the trees like Hansi Durmann, he wisely kept his counsel. Durmann had been Loring's best friend.

It's probably not even the same damn type of aeroplane, Zürst thought with resignation as he followed his flight leader into a steep, curving dive towards the offending woods. Loring had become obsessed.

I'm not going to kill myself just because you want revenge, Zürst thought as he plummeted behind Loring.

'Here they come!' Silverdale shouted. 'Take cover!'

He hunched in his seat, knowing the men and the young woman would be moving swiftly out of the line of fire of the attacking aircraft. He watched along his sights as the rapidly descending specks grew frighteningly large with each passing fraction of a second. He could scarcely believe it, but the nose-up attitude that had been given to the Lysander by sinking its tail in the depression appeared to be working perfectly. The leading 109E was filling the sights nicely.

It was definitely lower this time; much lower. Its pilot was clearly determined not to miss again and was prepared to take the additional risk of coming closer to the trees. Silverdale found himself thinking quite clinically that the German was pushing things beyond the edge. *Better for me if he's going beyond reason.*

He forced himself to wait. There was only the one chance, as he'd said.

Zürst felt uneasy as he plunged towards the wood, seemingly tied to Loring's aircraft. Zürst was very good at holding formation.

But something was wrong. Something had changed.

In the fleeting moments that drew the wood perilously closer, he realized what it was. *The target aircraft had moved.* They would have to realign. The earlier passes had been risky enough, but this was going to be positively dangerous. The aircraft on the ground was not worth the destruction of two valuable fighters.

Loring was going even lower. Even though they could see it, did he realize the aircraft was no longer in the same position? Did he realize that the pull-up would take them almost into the branches?

Zürst decided this was madness, and shifted position.

At that moment Loring had glanced back to check on his wingman's position.

'Zürst!' he rasped. 'You're out of line. Get back in!'

Glancing back would turn out to be a fatal mistake.

Even as he waited for the first signs of fire from the enemy aircraft, Silverdale watched in amazement as the lead Messerschmitt came ever lower.

He's not going to pull out in time, he thought in shock, and began to wonder whether he was now in greater peril of being hit by the aircraft itself. In seconds that seemed to stretch for ever, he saw that the number two was already aborting the attack, clearly deciding that the risk was far too high.

Now or never, Silverdale decided, and fired.

The tracers from the Lysander had barely started arcing towards the 109E when the enemy aircraft began spitting flame. A brief cluster of shells hit the ground then stopped abruptly. Silverdale stared wide-eyed as he continued to fire a burst that seemed longer than it actually was, his tracers appearing to be absorbed by the Messerschmitt. The approach speed would have given the shells and bullets even more destructive impact. The 109E rocked violently and pitched upwards viciously.

It barely skimmed the trees, trailing smoke, and Silverdale found himself ducking involuntarily as it screamed above the canopy. To Silverdale, it seemed almost as if the aircraft had itself made a sound of pain. Then a sudden explosion that flamed the woods some distance away made the ground shake. The Lizzie had scored her second kill. Good old Lizzie.

He heard shouting and turned to look, suddenly realizing he'd been holding his breath.

The young woman was at the side of the aircraft grinning hugely up at him.

'*Magnifique! Magnifique*, you crazy man!'

Her bodyguards were there, looking less dour. Their faces weren't going to crack into sudden smiles, but he supposed it was an improvement.

He reached to his right and pulled something away from a bracket, then leaned across to his left.

'Your present,' he said, and dangled the object outside the cockpit. 'As I promised.'

The 'present' turned out to be a brand-new, US Army-issue Thompson sub-machine-gun, complete with spare magazines taped to it. The 'Chicago piano' had grown respectable. It had been given to him as a present by an American he'd unexpectedly been sent to pick up. Unexpected because he'd had no idea that American agents were already involved in the war at such an early stage. From the very little he'd gleaned from his passenger, it dawned on him that a few of these agents had been in the field since the late thirties.

Her eyes widened with pleasure like a child being given the Christmas present of her dreams.

'Aah!' she began. 'A tommy-gun! I have heard of them . . . but to have my own! Aah . . .' she repeated, keen to take the weapon. Then she hesitated. 'But you cannot do this. It is yours!'

'Keep it for me until I see you again.'

She took the gift eagerly, caressing it in wonder, before displaying it to her companions. She gave her old Sten to one of them.

'This will not jam on me like the Sten,' she said to her colleagues in French, 'at the worst possible times.'

The simply constructed Sten, while a handy rapid-fire weapon that was widely used, did sometimes jam when you least wanted it to. She'd had two close shaves already. On the last occasion, only the quick reactions of the Resistance man who had been with her had saved her life. The gun had jammed while she'd been firing at a motorcycle patrol they'd run into. The one in the sidecar had a perfect shot on her with his mounted machine-gun. She could still see his grin of triumph. Then his mouth had opened wide in shock and a bloom of red had spilled out of it. He never saw the man who'd shot him.

She was reminding one of the men of the incident.

He was the one who'd shot the trooper. He was also in love with her, though she did not reciprocate. It was he who had stared hardest at Silverdale. Now he looked up from the weapon to the British pilot, his expression neutral.

'If I may interrupt,' Silverdale told him. 'You can admire it later. I'd like to get out of here.' He smiled at the young woman.

'Of course!' she said quickly and instructed the men to help push the aircraft out.

With judicious use of power, getting out of the depression was relatively easy. He rapidly went through his take-off checks, using the TMP mnemonic.

T – set *t*ail actuating wheel pointer to take-off; M – *m*ixture control to normal; P – push prop *p*itch control in for fine setting of the propeller; fuel on, gills open. He was ready.

The young woman ran to the side of the aircraft, and with a hand gripping the beret in place against the propwash, she called up at him.

'I would like to kiss you for the tommy-gun!'

'Do that when I see you again.'

'OK!' she promised with a shy smile.

'What do they call you?'

'We don't need names,' she replied. She tapped the Thompson. 'I have your gun.'

'Then use it to keep you safe.'

'I will!' she promised.

Silverdale waved at her and opened the throttle as she moved out of the way.

As the Lysander accelerated towards take-off speed, he did not raise the tail. Apart from the risk of smashing the prop into the ground, it was unnecessary. The Lizzie would virtually fly itself off. Then he would go into a steep emergency climb to clear the trees before heading back for the deck. He had to get out of there fast. No telling what the other Messerschmitt might be up to.

The Lizzie flew off well before the indicated speed had reached 80mph. He held the stick back and the aircraft climbed steeply, well beyond the stall of most other aeroplanes, at an indicated 70mph.

The four Resistance fighters watched as the aircraft appeared to stand on its tail as it lifted itself over the screen of trees. From within the woods, tracers began reaching for it but miraculously, it remained unharmed.

'Leave him, filthy Boche!' the young woman yelled pointlessly in her language. Even if they could have heard her over the firing, their most likely response would have been to target her as well.

The hard man who had stared at Silverdale had been studying her enigmatically as she had given the departing Lysander a little wave.

Then she gasped as a wing dipped suddenly and the aircraft lost height in a sickening drop that took it out of sight below the treetops.

'They have hit him!' she cried softly as the Lizzie disappeared.

But the fearfully expected explosion did not come. Even the tracers had stopped as the German gunners clearly thought they had scored and were waiting for confirmation. But in the ensuing silence, the sound of the Lysander's Mercury XX came through strongly.

She gave a little hop and laughed. 'He is too good for them! The package is safely on its way to England.'

'Is it only the package you are worried about, Mouflet?' the hard man asked.

'Mouflet' was slang for kid. Because she'd looked so young when she'd joined the group, everyone had simply called her the Kid. When she'd been given command, her code-name inevitably became Mouflet.

'What are you saying, Antoine?' she now asked. She was still looking at the spot where the aircraft had vanished.

'You know what I am saying.'

The other men watched them with interest. Everyone knew how Antoine felt about Mouflet. Everyone also knew exactly how *she* felt.

'Don't be ridiculous!' she said. 'I don't know the man.'

She did not look at him when she said this. As far as he was concerned, it was an answer that spoke volumes and he did not like it.

'Give the signal for our withdrawal,' she ordered, firmly closing the subject. 'We're finished here.'

'Fire the flare, Clavier,' Antoine instructed one of the others, saying the name with particular glee.

Clavier was not called thus because of his piano playing, but because, despite being in his late twenties, he had a mouthful of false teeth. At that moment in time, because of the way he felt about Mouflet and Silverdale, Antoine – older and with every tooth intact – wanted to take his frustration out on someone. Clavier was convenient.

With commendable affability, Clavier, who understood perfectly well what was going on in Antoine's mind, fired the green flare.

As it arced upwards everyone – including the Germans – could see. The Resistance fighters, no longer bound to their mission, swiftly disengaged and made their escape in small, widely dispersing teams along well-prepared routes. They took those of their dead who were still recognizable, and their wounded, with them.

The Germans in the woods, suddenly finding they had no one to fight any more, stared about them wonderingly. It was as if their foes had vanished into thin air, after inflicting heavy casualties on them. Their commander raged at the failure to secure the package, and vowed to make some harmless village pay. He knew his own head was on the block for this fiasco.

Mouflet and her men also made good their escape, splitting into pairs. Clavier went with her.

After his spectacular dive for the deck, Silverdale had levelled out to head back at low level for England. He wondered whether he would see those bright eyes again. He put the young Frenchwoman out of his mind and began to wonder about the second Messerschmitt. What was it up to? He couldn't see it anywhere, despite his extra vigilance.

He continued to scan around him for signs of the remaining enemy aircraft giving chase; but so far it had not put in an appearance.

There were some tracer holes from the ground fire in the Lizzie's wings, but nothing vital had been hit. He'd made it. The bloody package had made it, and the Lizzie now had two kills to its name.

The thought of his score reminded him of 'Bob' Shilling, and he found himself once more wondering about his friend's own tally. Was he getting the kills?

* * *

The reason Silverdale had received no further attention from the remaining 109 was because Leutnant Zürst was heading for base. Zürst was furious that Loring had allowed his obsession to kill him. Even if his flight leader had managed to destroy the aircraft, there would have been no chance of a successful pull-up before hitting the trees.

He would be brutally frank, Zürst decided, when he made his report after landing. Loring had been incredibly stupid.

3

Despite the daylight, Silverdale made it back without further incident. While he was on final approach to the Norfolk airfield where he was stationed, far to the north Shilling was staring at the place which would be his home for the coming months. Close to the sea, it looked even bleaker than he'd imagined.

His expression was one of pure dismay.

Creddon, who had negotiated the twisting, icy roads like a master of the art of winter driving, glanced at him.

'Cheer up, Sarge,' Creddon said, not unkindly. 'It's not as bad as it looks. The sea looks ugly now, but this is quite a beautiful place in the summer.' If you live long enough to see it, he thought sympathetically.

As he spoke, a pair of Hurricanes roared upwards into a thin curtain of snowflakes. Shilling tried to follow them with his eyes, leaning partially out of the car window to do so, at last seemingly oblivious of the cold. The tumbling flakes spattered his face, temporarily giving him a polka-dot complexion before melting on the relative warmth of his skin.

'You'll get your chance soon enough, Sarge,' Creddon told him as they turned the last corner into the approach road to the station gate. 'That was the CO and his number two going off, by the way. Bit of luck for you. You'll be meeting the deputy CO first. Good bloke. And close that window, please, Sarge. It's bloody cold in here.'

'Oh. Sorry.' Shilling wound the window shut. 'How do you know it was the CO?'

'He always takes this patrol. Usually flies three a day. One at this time, one in mid-afternoon and one at night about ten. Rain or shine, snow or wind, or wind and snow, he never changes the routine. The day he doesn't, we'll all know something's up . . . or he's bought it.'

'A man of habit.'

'Not exactly. He's split his day so he can handle other things.'

'When does he sleep?'

'He gets his sleep. And here we are. Welcome to your new home, Sarge.'

As they stopped at the gate and two armed sentries came forward, Shilling looked at the collection of snow-covered buildings and did not feel at all welcome.

The sentries looked unfriendly in their greatcoats and helmets, and carried their Sten guns at the ready. They were RAF ground gunners. Their boots crunched menacingly on the partially cleared snow. They split with synchronized timing to come to each side of the car, and one of them peered in.

This close, Shilling realized that the man was older than he'd first appeared; at least as old as Creddon.

'New pilot, Jimbo,' Creddon said easily to the sentry with a familiarity that the man accepted.

Jimbo stared at Shilling, eyes disbelieving. 'Are you trying it on with me, mate?'

'God's truth, Jimbo. And show some respect. He's a sergeant.'

Jimbo stared pointedly at the sergeant's chevrons on Shilling's greatcoat. 'So he is. Welcome to RAF Fort Town, Sergeant, home of the snow squadron. That's what we call it around here. Never known it not to snow.'

Shilling glanced quickly at Creddon. 'But Creddon says it's nice in the summer.'

'Oh it is, so they say. Haven't been here that long myself. Couldn't tell you.'

'Well, I'll just have to see what it's like when summer comes.'

He did not see the surreptitious glance that Creddon gave Jimbo, who turned to wave to two other sentries at the gate barrier. The barrier was raised.

'A beer later, Jimbo?' Creddon called as he began to drive slowly through.

'I could use one,' Jimbo replied as they passed, and the barrier was again lowered.

The four sentries resumed their guard positions.

'We'll book you in at the guardroom, Sarge, then I'll take you to the adjutant. He'll sort out the bumf with Station HQ. When he's finished with you, he'll introduce you to the deputy CO, Flight Lieutenant Johnstone. I'll be around to take you to the sergeants' mess, or what passes for it.'

He pulled up before the building near the gate which housed the RAF security personnel.

'Thanks,' Shilling said, 'but you don't really have to chauffeur me to the mess. I can walk it.'

'It's no bother. I've got a bit of time, anyway. Usually do after the drive from the train.'

'Thanks,' Shilling repeated as the car pulled up before the guardroom.

'Now let's wake up that dozy lot in there and get you booked in.'

*　　*　　*

When Shilling had been booked in and the car was driving away to the squadron, the sentry Creddon had called Jimbo stared after it.

'I give that poor bastard till spring,' he said to his companion. 'He'll never make it to summer.'

'Probably never make to spring,' the other man said philosophically. 'Never thought they'd let black people loose in aeroplanes, never mind fighters,' he went on. 'Bloody sergeant too. He outranks us.'

'Look at it this way. They could have made him an officer.'

'Never!' the sentry exclaimed, shocked.

'It's the war,' Jimbo remarked. 'Sends people barmy.'

As they drove towards the squadron buildings, Creddon said, 'It will be all over the station soon.'

'What will?'

Creddon gave Shilling a sly glance. 'Come on, Sarge. You know what I mean.'

'Do I?'

Creddon looked exasperated. 'Course you do. You're the only sergeant pilot on the squadron. You're the only *black* person most of those up here will have seen in RAF uniform . . .'

'There'll be more.'

'Perhaps, Sarge, but for now you're the only black *sergeant* anyone will have seen . . . me included.

You're the only black *pilot* most of the whole Air Force would ever have heard about, and you're the only black *fighter* pilot anyone . . .'

'I think I've got the message.'

'Well, then. As I said, it will be all over the station by the time Jimbo and that lot at the guardroom have used the bush telegraph . . . sorry. Didn't mean anything . . .'

'It's all right,' Shilling assured Creddon. 'I never use the bush telegraph myself.' He kept a straight face while Creddon peered at him.

'We get all sorts of squadrons up here from time to time,' Creddon went on, still unsure of Shilling's remark. 'They change over quite quickly.'

Now they were actually on the station and Shilling officially booked in on the unit strength, Creddon had become more informative.

'Had a Canadian bunch here not so long ago,' he continued. 'Lots of kills from their last posting.'

'How did they do up here?'

'Not so good. Not a lot of trade. Everyone thinks Jerry might still try an invasion anywhere, despite the beating in the air we gave him last year. But so far, only a few Ju-88s have come out to play. The Canadians took off to better hunting grounds. Then the snow squadron came. Been here ever since.'

'Any kills?'

'A few, but not as much as the CO would like.

He's got two Ju-88s . . . well one, really . . . had to share the second with his number two that day, Flying Officer Chivers. Then Flight Lieutenant Johnstone got an 88 and one of its escorts, an Me-110. You know, those twin-engined Messerschmitts.'

'Yes. I know.'

'Then another 88 came nosing around, with 109s as escorts. They ran into four of the squadron's Hurricanes. The 88 got away in cloud – plenty of that about in this part of the world – but two of the 109s went down. But we also lost a new boy that day. You're his replacement.

'We're still one pilot short, though,' Creddon continued, warming to his theme. 'Lost that one in a crash. He was trying to land in a snowstorm and missed all three runways completely, and even the emergency grass strip. As you'll find out, we get some stiff breezes – as the CO likes to call them – up here. Brass monkeys would hate it. I hate it, sometimes. No Waafs, either. Mark you, my missus wouldn't like to know I was on a station with Waafs. Thinks they're man-hungry.'

Shilling wondered what kind of Waaf would go chasing Creddon and was fascinated by that thought.

'No obstructions to speak of near the runways,' Creddon was saying, 'but he managed to hit that sea wall you saw on our way in. And that's the squadron score so far on this station. Most of the time the patrols come back without sighting anything.'

Shilling absorbed this information with foreboding. Snowstorms, sea walls, stiff breezes, the rare Ju-88. It looked as if he wouldn't even get the chance of a kill in this miserable place, after all. Plenty of trade would have been some consolation for being sent here, to the bleak far end of the country. But even that, it seemed, had been denied him.

He wanted to *fight*. Why hadn't they realized that?

'And here we are, Sarge,' Creddon said, bringing the car to a sliding halt. 'The snow squadron. The adj is Flying Officer Michaels. He's been recommissioned so he's a bit older than almost everybody else. He was a squadron leader then and sometimes still thinks he is. But don't let that put you off. He's a good bloke really. He was also a pilot in the twenties and early thirties, but he doesn't fly any more. One arm. Lost the other one in the Middle East somewhere. Iraq, I think. Um . . . when he's had a bit of the wet stuff he likes talking about the time he was fighting the fuzzy-wuzzies . . . but he probably won't say that in front of you . . .' Creddon paused awkwardly.

'You seem to know a lot,' Shilling said mildly.

Creddon grinned. 'Not much gets by me. Now

off you go, Sarge. See you back here later when you're ready for the mess.'

Shilling climbed out, hauled out his kit, then stuck out a hand. 'Thanks for everything.'

Creddon stared at the hand for a moment, then surprised himself by shaking it. 'Just doing my job, Sarge. One pilot delivered. See you later.'

The car whined and slid as Creddon turned it round.

As the sound of the engine faded, Shilling stamped his feet to clear the snow from his boots, then, with his bag over his shoulder, stepped into the hut that was the squadron headquarters. Constructed from cellular concrete, the hut felt warmer, but not much. A single corridor ran down its middle, with doors lining either side.

One swung ajar, and an administrative aircraft-man stepped out. He stared open-mouthed at Shilling.

'I'm Sergeant Shilling,' Shilling said, introducing himself to the staring airman. 'The new pilot.'

The airman continued to gape for so long Shilling feared they were going to be standing there in a frozen tableau for ever.

At last, sounds began to come from the airman.

'Er . . . er, yes . . . yes . . . S-S-Sergeant. You'd . . . you'd better see the adjutant, Fly . . . Flying Officer M-Michaels. P-Please follow me, Sergeant.'

Shilling trailed behind the airman.

Three doors on the right later, they passed one stencilled with white lettering. 'SQUADRON LEADER P. A. du TOIT, DFC, Officer Commanding,' it announced. The next one down proclaimed: 'FLIGHT LIEUTENANT HAMISH JOHNSTONE, DFC, AFC, Deputy Officer Commanding.' The third carried the legend 'FLYING OFFICER T. M. MICHAELS, DSO, Adjutant.'

All these decorations, he thought, wondering if he would ever get one.

The airman had stopped at the adjutant's door. He knocked once.

'Enter!' came an imperious voice.

The airman entered. 'S-Sir . . . th-the new p-pilot is h-here.'

'Show him in! And good God, Layson, when did you develop that stammer?'

'S-Stammer, sir?'

'Well, don't just stand there, man! Pilots are precious. Show him in!'

'Yessir!' The airman popped his head out like a burrowing animal scenting the air for danger. 'If you'll come in, please, Sergeant.'

'They sent us a *sergeant*?' came from within. 'Where are we going to put him?'

'The sergeants' mess, sir?' Layson suggested reasonably, glancing nervously into the room.

'There are no pilots in the sergeants' mess, Layson. The man will be on his own. Can't have that. You know what the CO thinks of his pilots.'

'Er . . . yes, sir.'

'We'll have to think of something.'

'Yes, sir.'

At that moment Shilling entered, put down his kitbag and came smartly to attention. He saluted the man behind the desk.

A deafening silence descended upon the small, basic office. Michaels did not gape as widely as Layson, but he came a close second.

Michaels was a thin man, though he did not have a small frame. Shilling decided it was the dreadful shock of the wound that had cost him his right arm, that had caused the unnatural thinness.

At last Michaels spoke. 'Good . . . Lord!' He stared disbelievingly at Shilling. 'Good bloody Lord!' he added as an extra measure.

He rose slowly from his chair. He was as tall as Shilling expected, almost gangly. He leaned slightly towards the missing arm, as if to balance himself. Thinning dark hair and a thin, dark moustache, very dark eyes, hooded by years of pain from his wound, all contributed to the haunted look about him. Shilling could understand why the adjutant sometimes took to drink. The eyes stared with unnerving blankness at the young sergeant.

'So. You are Shilling.'

'Yes, sir.'

'The signal gave us no rank, and no . . . description. At ease. Got your documents?' Michaels now looked troubled.

'Yes, sir.'

Shilling unbuttoned his greatcoat, undid a single button on his tunic and pulled out a large envelope. He buttoned his clothes once more, then handed the documents to Michaels.

The adjutant sat down, opened the envelope and began to study the contents. Shilling and Layson stood by, waiting for him to finish.

'Impressive,' Michaels commented, not looking up. 'Stand easy, Sergeant. Relax.'

Shilling relaxed.

'Your instructors have a very high opinion of you,' Michaels went on. 'Excellent pilot material seems to be the general consensus. You handle the Hurricane well. According to the instructors, you're not only a very good pilot, you also appear to have as instinct for air combat. We need both those qualities up here.' He looked up. 'I can study the rest later. The question that exercises my mind, Sergeant Shilling, is what to do with you.'

'I don't understand, sir.'

'I know you don't.' Michaels turned to Layson.

'All right, Layson. Find the sergeant a bed in the sergeants' mess, for the time being.'

'Yes, sir. I'll get on with it right away.' Layson left hurriedly.

'This is going to set the cat among the pigeons,' Michaels said, virtually to himself. 'Know anything about the CO, Sergeant?'

'Only the name I was told when I got the posting, sir. Free French?'

Then Shilling remembered Creddon's reaction to that same query. What would Michaels' be?

'*French?*' Michaels gave a hollow laugh. 'The family was, generations ago, certainly. But not today. Squadron Leader du Toit . . . is from South Africa, and hates the cold probably as much as you do.' The dark, hooded eyes stared very hard at Shilling. 'There the similarity ends.' Michaels gave no further clues to what was on his mind.

Shilling began to recall Creddon's words to him about the CO during the long drive, and felt a deep sense of foreboding.

'The CO will want to see you, of course,' Michaels continued briskly, 'when he returns from patrol. So keep yourself at the ready. I should be showing you off to Hamish Johnstone, the Deputy CO, but he's off to the officers' mess. In the meantime, get a hot meal inside you. You look as if you could use it.'

'Yes, sir. Thank you, sir.'

'All right, Sergeant, that is all for the moment. Layson will sort out your billet.' Michaels stood up once more and held out his left hand. 'Welcome to the snow squadron.'

Shilling shook the hand. 'Thank you, sir.' Then he saluted and turned to go.

'And Sergeant . . .'

Shilling looked round.

'Good luck up there.'

'Thank you, sir.'

When Shilling had gone, Michaels sat down slowly.

'Dear God,' he muttered. 'What malign idiot selected this posting for this poor boy?'

He reached into a drawer and took out a hip-flask covered in brown leather made shiny by years of use. He stared at it for some moments, then began to unscrew the stopper with great reverence.

'Good luck, boy,' he said, raising the flask in a toast. 'You're going to need it.' He brought the flask to his lips and took a generous swallow, sighed appreciatively, screwed back the stopper and returned the flask to its hiding-place.

'Aah!' he said again, and belched. 'There was a time when I was surrounded by fuzzy-wuzzies . . .' He stopped, and rubbed the stump of the missing arm reflectively.

Then he got the flask out again and took another swig, before putting it back and slamming the drawer shut.

'Damn it!' he growled. 'They sent that boy up here to die . . . or they're hiding him.'

Shilling was standing outside the squadron hut when the car came sliding to a halt.

Creddon got out, leaving the engine running. 'All finished, are we, Sarge?'

'Yes.'

'Sergeants' mess, is it?'

Shilling nodded.

'Right. Hop in. Been talking to a corporal mate of mine who looks after arrangements there. He'll see you're all right. Get you a nice billet.'

'Do you know everybody in this place?' Shilling said as he got into the car.

Creddon climbed in behind the wheel. 'Just about.'

'Well?' Shilling began as they started off. 'Is it all over the station?'

'Your arrival? It is. News gets round fast.'

'Bad news, you mean?'

'I didn't say that, Sarge,' Creddon said, quickly defensive.

'It's the feeling I have,' Shilling told him. 'The adjutant was shocked to see me, as was Layson.

67

They didn't bother to hide it and just didn't say anything for a while.'

In the awkward silence that followed, Creddon said, 'Look, Sarge. I shouldn't be saying this, but . . . just watch your step with the CO.'

'Because he comes from South Africa? The adj told me.'

'That's part of it,' Creddon replied guardedly. 'A big part.'

'And the rest?'

'That's all I'm saying, Sarge. I've said enough as it is.'

Creddon dropped Shilling off at the sergeants' mess and drove off to one of the other ranks' barrack huts. A group of men were huddled round one of the two cast-iron stoves installed along the centreline of the hut.

'Dropped off your darkie, Two-Wheel?' one of them greeted.

They all called him Two-Wheel Creddon because of the way he drove. The mythology was that when driving at his craziest he took corners on two wheels. Many even thought he'd have made a passable racing driver if he'd been born with the right privileges.

'Ooohh . . . there was a young lady from . . .' another began to sing.

'Not that again!' someone else interrupted with a groan. 'Sing anything else, Nobby. You've done it twice already.'

But Nobby, an excellent aircraft mechanic who'd continued singing in a terrible voice, was not to be deflected, creating his own version of the limerick.

'. . . who had an affair with a daaarkie . . . when the babies were boorn . . . she screamed . . . "Oh . . . my . . . gawn . . ."' ·

'". . . *one black, one white and one khaki!*"' the rest of them chorused, then burst into fits of laughter.

Creddon, who had not joined in, stared at them. 'So you all think it's funny?'

'Come on, Two-Wheel,' Nobby began. 'They must have known what he'd have to put up with, sending him here.'

But Creddon had undergone a transformation, from passive racist to champion of the underdog.

'He's a *sergeant, and* a pilot. He's going to be up there, up to his neck in Jerries while you lot are safe down here . . .'

'Jerry doesn't come out to play much these days . . .'

'Got that direct from Lord Haw-Haw in Germany, did you, Chalky?' Creddon glared at the speaker. 'For God's sake, all of you. He's just a kid! He's far from home, he's got no friends, and he could die any day. He's also doing something none of you can do. Be decent for once in your lives. Treat the kid proper.'

They were all staring at him.

'What's got into you?' Chalky White demanded. 'You used to laugh at the darkies in those Tarzan movies like the rest of us.'

Creddon looked embarrassed. 'Well, he's not like that,' he replied gruffly. 'Polite too. He even shook my hand to thank me for picking him up. None of the other pilots ever did that.'

Creddon walked out, leaving them staring bewilderedly at his departure.

Creddon's corporal friend was as good as promised. The sleeping accommodation in the sergeants' mess hut was partitioned into small, enclosed, two-bed sections but with no ceiling, to allow the heat from the ubiquitous, centrally placed stoves to warm them.

'There you are, Sarge,' the corporal said. 'Got you a nice corner room all to yourself. It's one of the warmest ones – close to a stove. As a pilot, you get more space.'

'Thanks, Corp,' Shilling said, not certain whether it was because he was a pilot or because no one wanted to share with him. He didn't mind, and preferred it that way.

'You need anything, Sarge,' the corporal went on, 'just let me know.'

Shilling nodded. 'I'll remember that. Seems Creddon's as good as his word.'

The corporal smiled crookedly. 'Old Two-Wheel's a champion bloke. He was here when Layson called to say you were coming.'

'"Two-Wheel"? Is that what you call him?'

The corporal explained.

'I can believe that,' Shilling remarked drily, remembering his recent drive.

The corporal smiled again. 'Everyone he picks up remembers that trip from the station. You're late for breakfast,' he went on, 'and early for lunch, but I've organized something for you. So when you're ready, the cooks have got some nosh waiting in the dining hut.'

'Thanks again, Corp. I'll just get my kit sorted out and be right over.'

'Right, Sarge.'

'Oh, and what's your name?'

'Billings.'

Shilling held out his hand. Surprised, Billings hesitated, then shook it, a bemused expression slowly forming on his face.

'Right, Sarge,' he said.

When the helpful corporal had gone, Shilling entered his cubicle and put the kitbag on the spare bed, then he sat down on the other and looked about him. There were two standard-issue utility beds, and beside them two wooden lockers with blankets for both beds neatly piled on top of them.

'Well, I won't be cold at night,' he said to himself.

Outside, one of the 'stiff breezes' that Creddon had mentioned was winding itself up for a good blow and whistled against the hut.

It sounded as lonely as he felt.

The food was surprisingly good, and welcomingly hot. Shilling was the only person in the eating area of the dining hut, but he knew the cooks were surreptitiously watching him. He had just finished the meal and was sipping his tea when an officer entered.

Shilling began to get to his feet.

The officer stopped him. 'Please carry on, Sergeant Shilling,' he said pleasantly as he came up. 'Mind if I join you?'

'No. No, sir.' Shilling saw the two blue rings on the officer's shoulders. This must be Johnstone, he realized.

'As you've no doubt concluded,' the flight lieutenant said, taking the chair opposite, 'I'm Johnstone, Deputy CO.'

'I'd have come over, sir, as soon as I'd finished eating.'

Johnstone smiled thinly. 'Very correct young man, aren't you? This is on my way back to the squadron hut, so it was no trouble.' He raised his voice. 'How long do I have to wait for a mug of tea?'

'Coming up, sir!' a voice replied.

'The tea here's better than at our mess,' Johnstone confided to Shilling. 'I always stop off whenever I get the opportunity. I think it's all a plot,' he went on with good humour. 'After all, it is the senior NCOs who recommend the cook allocations to the catering officer.'

Shilling gave a hesitant smile.

'Since time immemorial,' Johnstone continued, 'the SNCOs have been the real power in the land of the military. Who ran Caesar's armies if not the centurions? You've no doubt by now made a thorough acquaintance of our hell-on-wheels driver?' he added.

'Yes, sir. He seems to know just about everything and everyone.'

'Don't know how he does it, but he does indeed seem able to get the gen before anyone else. Pure gold, of course. A handy man to have around.'

While Johnstone had been speaking, Shilling had allowed his eyes to stray towards the line of medal ribbons beneath the Deputy CO's wings.

'Were you in the Battle, sir?'

Johnstone glanced down at his decorations. 'After some of those yourself?'

'Not as a goal, sir, but I am keen to get into combat.'

'I'm sure you are. You're all keen ... in the beginning. Yes, I was in the Battle, and in France too. I saw a few keen ones go down before they'd scored a single kill. It's not a game out there, young Bob. I suppose everyone calls you Bob?'

'Yes, sir.'

'Inevitable. My name's Hamish when we're not on ceremony. As you can tell, I don't have a Scottish accent. Transplanted I may be, but I'm still a Scot, even though I do like my tea.'

Before Shilling could make comment, one of the cooks brought Johnstone's tea. 'Just as you like it, sir. Hot, milky and sweet.'

'Aah. I thought I'd have to wait for ever. Thank you, Nichols.'

'Sir.'

'Settling in all right?' Johnstone carried on to Shilling when Nichols had gone.

'Yes, sir. I've got a nice warm room.'

'Good. Good. Tends to be brass-monkey weather most of the time during this half of the year. I'm sorry you're going to be all on your own. We have no other sergeant pilots. Expected an officer, you see. If I had my way I'd make special arrangements to have you in with us; but I know the CO won't wear it. But I will try to see if you can at least eat with us. We can obey protocol by making you our frequent guest. Seems rather long-winded to me, but there it is.'

'Yes, sir.

'Mad Mikey the adj informs me you've got excellent reports from your instructors.'

'I was lucky, sir.'

'Lucky, my foot! By all accounts, they were singing your praises. Never been on the Hurricane II?'

'No, sir. All my Hurricane time is on the Mark I.'

'You'll soon get the hang of it. We've got the newest of the new IICs with the 1280hp Merlin 20 engine, *and* four Hispano 20mm cannon to boot, instead of the eight .303 machine-guns. We're probably the first squadron so equipped. We've also got the new three-bladed, constant-speed propeller. You'll find her as steady a gun platform as your old mount but even more devastating, and all the important controls are identical. The change-over should not give you too much trouble.'

Johnstone took an enjoyable swallow of the tea and went on, 'We're down from 345 to about 340mph with the cannon, but in the dive we're nearer 400 instead of 390. Use that extra diving speed to give you zoom energy. It always catches

Jerry by surprise. I've seen 410 on the clock, so in certain circumstances you may be able to push for that little extra. It could save your life.'

Shilling listened avidly, soaking up the wisdom of the veteran before him. Johnstone was younger than he'd expected, but the eyes were those of an old man. Stocky, with cropped brown hair, the 'transplanted' Scot had a squarish but pleasant face. The hands seemed heavy, almost ploughman's hands; yet, Shilling decided, they must have a delicate sense of control. Proof were the decorations adorning Johnstone's chest. Better proof was the fact that Johnstone was still alive. Shilling did not know it then, but Johnstone was just twenty-two and a half.

'So tell me,' Johnstone was saying, 'how would you like to be introduced to your new steed?'

'I would, sir!'

'That's the spirit. No time like the present. Let's see if those instructors had all their marbles in one place when they gave you those glowing reports. The CO won't be back for a while yet, so how about you and I checking to see what's above the clouds?'

'I'm with you, sir!'

Johnstone took another gulp of tea. 'Mind you don't bring up your lunch. I'll be asking you to follow me through some interesting manoeuvres.'

'I'll keep my lunch, sir.'

The thin smile came back. 'Very well, Bob Shilling. Dispersal in half an hour. Your aircraft will have the letter-code B for Baker after the fuselage roundel. Or B for Bob, if you prefer. Oh yes ... when you stop off at Stores for your new flying kit, get yourself some new flying boots as well. They're a new issue, and stronger and warmer than the ones you've no doubt brought with you. You'll need them up here.'

'Yes, sir!'

Johnstone stood up and stopped Shilling, who was about to do likewise. 'Finish your tea before it gets any colder. Keen,' he added as he went out. 'Very keen.'

4

Within minutes of Johnstone's departure, Shilling looked up and saw Creddon approaching. The driver certainly appeared to have a sixth sense that was at a constant high state of readiness.

Creddon arrived at the long table and remained standing respectfully. 'All squared away, Sarge?'

'All sorted. Thanks for the help, Two-Wheel. Grab a chair.'

'It's all right, Sarge. I'll be going back to the car.' Then Creddon's eyebrows went up briefly. 'So the corp told you?'

'Yes.'

'I don't really deserve that name.'

Shilling smiled at him. 'You're stuck with it. Even the officers think of you like that.'

'Just my luck. I saw the Deputy CO leaving. You're going flying with him.' It was a statement born of factual knowledge.

'I am, and I've got to stop off and pick up some new boots when I get my kit.'

'Thought you might. They're the best boots around.'

'Don't tell me you've managed to get your hands on a pair.'

Creddon gave a discreet cough and said nothing.

'I wonder why I'm not surprised,' Shilling said drily. He was learning quickly.

'I'll be waiting in the car. Take you to Stores, then on to Dispersal.'

'That's kind of you.'

'Someone's got to look after you down here, Sarge,' Creddon said awkwardly. 'Up there, it's out of my hands.' He left the hut quickly, as if he didn't want to hear what Shilling would say to that.

Shilling watched him leave, touched by the man's new attitude.

Leutnant Zürst had not received the reaction he'd expected when he'd made his report concerning the incident with the Lysander.

His commanding officer, Oberstleutnant Hermann Steinhausen, had been less than pleased by his solitary return and had virtually accused him of cowardice, and of deserting his flight leader in the face of the enemy. He was not to know that

Steinhausen and Loring had been comrades during the Condor Legion's support of Franco in Spain. Loring had never told him.

'You may come from a powerful family, Zürst,' Steinhausen had yelled at him, 'but I will see to it that you never again serve in any command I may be given! For a long time, I have suspected that you are not at one with the Cause. Your kind of people brought Germany to its knees! It took the Führer to give us back our self-respect. So don't you stand there and tell me that Oberleutnant Loring was stupid to continue the attack! I knew Loring as a very brave man indeed. You should have backed him. That was your *duty*. You have just cost me one of my best pilots!'

Steinhausen had drawn a long breath, before continuing with his barrage. 'I may seem to you to have come from only a backwoods farming family, but I'll tell you, Zürst, our kind – mine and Loring's – are the future. You dilettantes are on the way out. I wish I had sufficient proof to have you court-martialled and *shot*! As I can't do that, I'll do my best to see that you get the worst postings imaginable. You are grounded! Now get out of here while I decide what to do with you!'

*   *   *

Shilling found that the new boots were indeed very warm, and comfortable.

With his winter warms beneath his clothes, he discovered he did not feel the cold so much as he trudged in his Mae West, with his packed parachute bumping along on his behind, towards the aircraft that Johnstone had selected for him. It was almost possible to forget the rawness of the wind that had sprung up. He decided it was the excitement of actually getting ready to fly that had so stimulated his adrenalin that he was oblivious to the cold.

If this chute doesn't work, the supply sergeant had said to him, come back and we'll give you another one. He'd heard *that* one before.

The runways had been cleared of snow, so there would be no worries about the take-off.

He came up to B for Baker and stopped. It looked big and shiny, gleaming aggressively in the cold Scottish light, its characteristic hump behind the birdcage cockpit making it seem mean and dangerous. This lethal appearance was augmented by the protruding snouts of the pair of cannon on each wing. He loved it on sight.

'Not too tired after your long trip?' a voice asked solicitously behind him.

He turned to see a fully kitted Johnstone. 'Not tired at all, sir!'

'Hmm. I can see by that gleam in your eye you're raring to go.'

'I am, sir!'

'All right, young man. Do your outside checks then hop aboard and familiarize yourself with the cockpit. I'll pop up to answer any questions you may have.'

Shilling went through the checks while Johnstone watched approvingly, then stepped up on the wing root, slid back the canopy, and climbed into the cockpit. Johnstone followed him, then paused against the cockpit to observe him at work.

Johnstone watched as Shilling's hands moved around the cockpit, reacquainting himself with the various controls and instruments, nodding in approval as he noted the confidence with which Shilling did so.

Shilling checked the idiosyncratically positioned undercarriage and flap levers on the right. Some things never changed.

'All seems fine here,' he said to Johnstone.

'So no questions so far. Good,' Johnstone said, then went on: 'Because we get such low temperatures hereabouts, we're using high-volatility fuel. Today we're at −10°C. This is relatively mild, so you'll need only eight or so strokes of the priming pump. With just a normal load of standard fuel, cannon and ammo, keep the trim neutral. There'll be two men to hold your tail down while you warm her up. Aircraftmen Clark and Coates. They look after my machine and are the best around here. I've instructed them to look after you.'

'Thank you, sir.'

'I'll accept your thanks when you show me what you can do. During part of this sortie I want you to stick to me like glue, no matter what manoeuvres I execute. Then at some stage I shall break formation without warning to feign an attack on you. You must look sharp and defend yourself. And please don't get too excited and shoot me down, old boy, should you be lucky enough to get on my tail.'

Shilling suppressed the smile he felt coming.

'Despite our little fun and games, keep a very sharp lookout for the Hun. He could put in an appearance at any time. Our stamping ground includes Scapa Flow, where he likes to make his visits to the ships, from bases in Occupied Holland and points north.' Johnstone gave him a brief pat on the shoulder. 'Now let's get you upstairs.'

Johnstone climbed down, and waited for Clark and Coates, who were approaching Shilling's aircraft.

'Remember what I said,' he told them. 'You will treat this aeroplane like my own.'

'Yes, sir,' they both acknowledged.

'Never thought I'd get *his* bloody plane,' Nobby

Clark grumbled as Johnstone left them. 'Bloody fate. That's what it is.'

'Shut up, for God's sake!' Bill Coates admonished him in a sharp whisper. 'He might hear you!'

'Who? The Deputy CO? Or him up there in the cockpit?'

'Either! Now get ready to hold down that tail.'

Having secured himself in the cockpit, Shilling, oblivious of Clark's rancorous mood, began his engine starting procedures.

Main tanks fuel cock to on. Throttle half an inch open. Supercharger control to 'moderate'. Radiator shutter open. Ignition on. Starter and booster coil buttons – push together – down there on the left, two-finger job. Prime engine while being turned. No more than twenty seconds at a time.

After eight strokes the engine started lustily first time. Shilling immediately released the starter button, then the booster button as the engine settled down. He screwed down the priming pump and opened the throttle slowly to 1000rpm to let the engine warm up.

When satisfied, he waved the men off and, after checking that both brake pressure and pneumatic supply pressure were OK, began to taxi. He saw that Johnstone's aircraft was already on the move.

He followed his flight leader to the runway

threshold, and did a rapid pre-take-off check. Rudder trim tab fully right to counter engine torque, elevator neutral, main tanks on, pressurizing cock to 'atmosphere', flaps 28° down, supercharger to 'moderate', radiator shutter fully open. He was ready. Johnstone was moving.

Shilling slid the canopy shut and pushed the throttle to the gate. The Hurricane surged forward, keeping pace with the rapidly accelerating Johnstone.

Shilling felt a supreme lifting of his spirits as the thunder reverberated through him. All else faded into a significance so minute, it might as well not have existed: his sense of isolation, the South African CO, the posting to this wilderness. Everything was as nothing compared with what he was now feeling. He wanted to sing with the engine. A big smile creased his face.

He raised the undercarriage in unison with Johnstone, then retrimmed the aircraft to nose-heavy. He kept close station with Johnstone as the speed built.

On the ground, Clark and Coates had watched the take-off.

'So he can take off,' Clark said grudgingly. 'They could probably teach Tarzan's monkey to fly.'

'So what does that make you? You can't fly.'

Clark turned to see Creddon standing behind him. Unable to counter, he ignored the question.

'The Deputy CO's ordered me to service B for Baker.' He sounded as if he'd been insulted. 'That's the one . . .'

'I know who's flying it, Nobby. Mind that you do a good job. If anything goes wrong you'll have me to deal with.'

'After me,' a hard voice said.

They all turned to see the flight sergeant in charge of servicing.

'See here, Nobby,' the senior NCO began. 'What our masters at the Air Ministry or wherever do, is nowt to do with us. And whether we like having a coloured sergeant here with us is not for discussion. He's flying His Majesty's Hurricane. He's wearing His Majesty's uniform. He's His Majesty's sergeant. He's in His Majesty's Royal Air Force. You have been given an order by one of His Majesty's officers. You will obey that order, or I'll break your sodding neck. *Got it?*'

'Ye-yes, Flight! Got it.'

The flight sergeant turned to Creddon. 'Why are you still here, Creddon?'

'Just leaving, Flight,' Creddon said hastily. 'Just leaving!'

*   *   *

At 140mph indicated airspeed, they were climbing through cloud to 16,000 feet. Shilling had switched on his formation-keeping floodlamps on the fuselage beneath the cockpit and the navigation lamps at the wingtips. He stayed close to Johnstone and was still close when they broke into bright sunlight out of the clouds.

He switched off the lamps, and looked across to his left. The other aircraft was so close that he could clearly see Johnstone's eyes as his flight leader looked back at him.

Johnstone led him into a series of punishing manoeuvres, snapping this way and that: rolling, climbing, looping. Shilling stayed glued.

'Your instructors have indeed got all their marbles in one place,' came over the radio. Johnstone sounded impressed.

Then he disappeared.

Shilling did a quick scan of the clear sky above the clouds and immediately broke tightly to his right. He remembered the flight sergeant instructor telling him that most pilots, especially the novices, tended to break left when going into an avoidance manoeuvre. The aces knew that and were always waiting to nail them.

'Break right,' the SNCO instructor had said. 'The ace may well know the move, but it will throw him off for vital moments. After that, it's up to your ingenuity and instincts. You've got both. Use them.'

As he broke and rolled into a dive, he saw that the instructor was right, after all. Johnstone had been powering down from the left rear quarter and the unexpected break had caught him completely by surprise.

'Oh ho!' Shilling heard on his headphones. 'That was a good one, young Bob. But can you keep away from me?'

Shilling had gained a 400mph airspeed in the dive and was now hauling hard against the forces of gravity in order to use one of Johnstone's own lessons and convert the speed into a zoom climb. But Johnstone would know that and expect it, so just as he was beginning the climb and still with plenty of speed, Shilling rolled hard into a 90° bank, breaking the climb momentarily, rolled level once more, still with good speed, and hauled the Hurricane into a loop.

At the top, he looked through his canopy and saw Johnstone on the way down to where Johnstone had expected him to be.

Shilling hauled the Hurricane as tightly as he could bear, and soon the nose was again plunging towards the clouds. He continued to pull, straining against the control forces. The nose began to rise, curving towards Johnstone's aircraft.

He was on Johnstone's tail!

He could scarcely believe his luck. Johnstone must have made it easy for him, he decided. But it didn't appear so. As he drew closer, it became apparent that the other man had temporarily lost sight of him, for taking no chances, Johnstone was not flying a predictable path for more than a few moments at a time.

Shilling, however, remained stuck to the hard-manoeuvring aircraft.

'Sticking like glue,' Shilling called.

Johnstone's exclamation was involuntary. 'I'll be damned! No one's ever done that to me, young Bob. If I'd been a Jerry, I'd be dead.'

'Roger, sir,' Shilling said.

'I owe you a pint in the mess. *Our* mess.'

'You're on.'

'Close in. We're going home. Well done.'

'Roger. Closing in . . . *Bandit, bandit! Three o'clock low!*'

A single Ju-88 was skimming the cloud bank 3000 feet beneath them. It must have just popped up, Shilling thought. He scanned the air about him quickly. Were there escorts?

He reached quickly for the cannon master switch ahead of the throttle lever and flicked it on, then reached low down to his left for the cocking lever and cocked the weapons. He was ready for combat. He felt elated.

'Eyes of a hawk,' Johnstone was saying. 'Aah! I've got him! Any escorts?'

'I'm looking . . . *yes, yes! Two! Five o'clock! High and coming down!*'

'Break!' Johnstone called. 'Go for that bomber! I'll keep the fighters off your back!'

'Roger!' Shilling called and rolled into a dive after the Ju-88.

Johnstone went into a shallow dive to gain more speed, then leapt for the descending fighters, which turned out to be Me-109s. They immediately adjusted their downward rush to counter the threat, leaving the bomber unprotected.

It was what Johnstone had hoped for. At that instant he broke the climb and headed down again, this time away from Shilling and the bomber. They followed. He wanted them down where the Hurricane performed best, at medium to low levels.

They kept coming.

Shilling was rapidly approaching the Ju-88. He knew from his recognition lectures that this aircraft would not necessarily be easy meat. Despite its size, the twin-engined 88 could manoeuvre reasonably well, and was also well armed with a rear gun behind the glasshouse cockpit, one firing above the nose ahead of the forward cockpit, plus a ventral gun firing to the rear. The pilot also sat in an armoured seat that protected his back.

Shilling decided to go for a head-on pass from above. If he could get his cannon shells into that cockpit quickly, it would cease to matter about the other guns.

Kill the pilot, he thought, astonishing himself by the coldly clinical manner in which he'd made the decision.

He went into a tight, curving turn that put him in a position that would give him a shallow approach to the right and a little above the enemy. By now his speed was again nearing the 400 mark.

They'd been watching out for him and the enemy pilot began to bank hard across his line in an attempt to defeat his aim and bring the rear guns to bear. But the manoeuvre had been started too late. The closing speeds were too high to allow escape.

The forward gun, put out of aim by the steep bank, fired uselessly. Shilling had the barest of moments in which to fire before he too lost his aim on that first pass. A second would be more dangerous, now that the enemy were fully alerted.

He fired.

The awesome sound and destructive power of the four-cannon onslaught astonished him. The 88 seemed to fly straight into the cone of fire as four streams of tracer converged at the exact spot where the cockpit had placed itself. The glasshouse shattered as shells exploded in a brief but terrible hell within the enemy cockpit.

The aircraft immediately nosed over and plunged towards the cloud bank as Shilling's Hurricane flashed past. There was no smoke, but that didn't necessarily mean anything.

He pulled up into a loop and on the way back down saw just the one parachute. The bomber had disappeared; then something flamed deep within the whiteness beneath him. The parachute, with its small-looking object dangling beneath, went into the cloud.

Shilling did not give much for the chances of survival of the unfortunate man at the end of that chute, in the freezing waters below.

For the barest moment he felt a twinge of remorse before remembering that Johnstone was in a tangle with two fighters. He went to look for his flight leader and almost immediately saw a smoke trail heading cloudwards. He heaved a sigh of relief when he saw a Hurricane racing towards him. Of the other Messerschmitt there was no sign.

'Did you get him?' Johnstone asked as they rejoined formation.

'Yes. I think it exploded in the clouds. I saw a bright-red glow. And I saw a chute.'

'Good man! You've been blooded on your first operational flight. I now owe you *two* beers!'

'And you?'

'Got one.'

'I saw.'

'The other chose discretion and fled for home. Let's do the same, shall we? Well done, young Bob!'

The squadron commander and his wingman landed while Johnstone and Shilling were still airborne.

Paul du Toit was a solid-looking man, taller than Johnstone, but not as tall as Michaels. Heavy, tanned features were topped by a head of fine blond hair which he wore parted in the middle. His eyes were so pale they appeared to mirror the northern winter, an unnerving vision that tended to startle those who met him for the first time. Moreover, they appeared to have nothing hidden within their depths.

He climbed out of his Hurricane and removed his helmet, looking fed up.

Creddon was waiting with the car. 'No trade, sir?'

'None whatsoever,' du Toit replied in his pronounced South African accent. 'Man, those damn Jerries are playing a cat-and-mouse game, or they're scared of coming out. I wish I could believe it's because they have given up.'

'It's not going to be over by Christmas this year either, is it, sir?'

'I'm afraid not.'

Creddon held the car door open. 'The mess, sir?'

'No. Take us to the squadron hut for debriefing, then you can drop Flying Officer Peters off at the mess.' Du Toit turned to glance back at the other Hurricane, whose pilot was just climbing out, before turning once more to Creddon. 'I assume you've picked up our new pilot?'

'Yes, sir,' Creddon replied guardedly.

Du Toit frowned, momentarily bemused by Creddon's tone, but made nothing of it for the time being. 'Has he settled in?'

'Yes, sir.'

'Where is he now?'

'Aloft, sir. Flight Lieutenant Johnstone took him up for the usual.'

As the squadron's acknowledged ace, with seven victories – now eight – a score that began with his time in France and the Battle of Britain, it was Johnstone's unofficial task to break in the new pilots.

'Nothing like throwing them in at the deep end to sort out the men from the boys,' du Toit remarked easily. 'If Mr Johnstone can't, no one can.'

'Yes, sir.'

Du Toit stared at Creddon. 'What's up with you,

man? Usually it's difficult to stop you chattering. Today it feels as if I am about to put you on the rack. Is there something I should know?' The pale eyes seemed to reach into Creddon's very bones, chilling him.

'I think I should leave that to the adj, sir.'

Now du Toit's frown had come back. 'I see,' he said in a voice that had grown suddenly cold. He turned to Peters, who was ambling along. 'Hurry it up, there!'

Peters hurried. 'Yes, sir!'

Du Toit got into the front of the car while Peters climbed in the back.

'All right, Creddon,' the squadron commander said.

Stony-faced, Creddon started off for the squadron hut.

'*A sergeant?*' du Toit exclaimed, looking annoyed. Michaels was in his office and had just given him the first part of the news about Shilling. 'They sent me a *sergeant*? I asked for officers. We have no sergeant pilots on the squadron. Billeting arrangements are . . .'

'We've put him in the sergeants' mess,' Michaels said, interrupting his CO. He could get away with it because, despite himself, du Toit sometimes unconsciously deferred to Michaels because of the other's combat history and former rank. 'But there's more, I'm afraid.'

'More? How could there be more? The man's a sergeant. What else can there be?'

'He's er . . . from the colonies.'

'So? I'm from a sort of colony.'

'Not what I'm really getting at, sir. You see . . . he's not . . . er from one of the white colonies . . .'

'What?' du Toit began softly. 'You mean they have sent a *black* man? To *my* squadron? To fraternize with *my* officers? Is this a joke? I want him transferred out of here immediately! Get the paperwork started.'

Michaels cleared his throat. 'If I may suggest, sir . . . it may take months before you succeed in having him moved, given the nature of such things. It is far more likely that the Hun will get him before the posting is authorized.'

'You're saying I should live with it?'

'I am saying, sir, that the powers that be had their own reasons for sending him here. They would not take kindly to your opposing their decision. It could have a somewhat . . . er . . . detrimental effect on one's career, if you see what I mean.'

The pale eyes fastened on Michaels. 'And that's your opinion?'

'For what it's worth . . . yes, sir.'

'I see.'

'Hamish had suggested,' Michaels went on tentatively, 'that as Shilling's rather isolated in the sergeants' mess, he ought to be mixing with his fellow pilots. Good for squadron morale. Regulations allow for us to invite him as a guest to dine with us . . .'

'*No!* I will not have it!'

'But sir . . . !'

Du Toit stared emptily at Michaels. 'May I remind you, Flying Officer Michaels, who is commanding officer here? Not you, not Johnstone, but *me*! Are you contesting that?'

Michaels waited just long enough before replying mildly, 'Of course not, sir.'

'Now do you see?' du Toit went on irritably. 'Do you see what they have done? We're arguing. By posting him here they have disrupted the equilibrium of the squadron. Someone somewhere must have thought, what do we do with this black sergeant pilot? Ah, du Toit! He's South African. He knows how to handle blacks. Do you see, man? They've slapped me in the face.'

'I wouldn't quite put it like that, sir. As I've said, I believe they have quite different motives . . .'

'Who cares? He's *here*, in *my* squadron. I'm the one saddled with the problem.'

If Michaels thought du Toit was making his

own problems, he chose to say nothing about it.

'*Verdomme!*' du Toit swore.

Michaels stared impassively at him.

I need a drink, Michaels thought wistfully.

5

Beyond any doubt, Susan Chandler was an astonishingly beautiful young woman. At eighteen, the bloom of her youth lent a special appeal to her emerging womanhood, making her irresistible to the male eye.

She was of average height, with long, gleaming, dark-brown hair. Her pale-brown eyes possessed such luminosity that any man could easily be fooled into believing that if he gazed into them deep enough he would find himself in another world.

Her body was athletic, and still carried the barest vestige of teenage puppy-fat. It made her even more alluring. Hers was a strong nose, sculpted sharply, with the slightest of inward curves. It suited perfectly the gentle oval of her face. However, it was to the eternal chagrin of all the young men who knew her that she showed no interest in them whatsoever, although when she was angry the skin about her nostrils tended to whiten. Currently, it was rapidly attaining that pallor.

'I *want* to do something for the war effort,' she was saying with an emphasis that was almost expected to be accompanied by the stamp of a foot; but Susan Chandler was not someone who stamped her foot. 'I could be a driver,' she insisted, adopting a more reasonable tone. 'I could join the Wrens, or the Waafs. I could . . .'

'No . . .' This from her father, a former Army general, now involved in aircraft production.

'But it just isn't fair! You're doing something. Timothy's in the RAF . . .'

'Precisely. Your mother will be left all alone. She hasn't been well for some time and the war does not help. She would be worried about all three of us. She needs you.'

'But Nurse Henderson . . .'

'Nurse Henderson comes when she can,' her father interrupted, 'but her other duties have become more onerous since this little disagreement with Herr Hitler began. You can be a companion to your mother and continue your studies here at the same time. When this is finally over, the nation will have need of educated young women. Things are changing. The country will not be returning to what it once was. Anyone who believes otherwise is a fool. It will not be a time for fools. Young people like you will be vital to the regrowth of the nation. Think about it, Susan.'

She was still hoping to change his mind and turned to her brother for help.

'Tim? Do you agree?'

Flying Officer Timothy 'Shippy' Chandler was a Hurricane pilot, and was spending a last few days with his family before taking up his new posting. Though his features were closer to the squarer ones of his father, his eyes were of the same colour as his sister's, and he was appreciably taller.

'Don't pull me into this, old girl,' he countered good-naturedly.

'You're a lot of help.'

He smiled fondly at her.

'Then it's settled,' their father said. 'I'll go up to say goodbye to your mother. When are you off, Tim?'

'Not for a day or two yet.'

'Then I may well be able to get back before you leave. We can all have dinner together, perhaps? No telling when we'll have the chance again.'

'I'll be here, Pop.'

'Wish you wouldn't call me by that American aberration. You've been mixing with those Eagle Squadron people.'

'Oh, they're a good bunch of chaps, our colonial cousins.'

'I'm sure they are. They're doing valuable work, and we do appreciate their coming over before the Americans are properly in the war.'

Tim Chandler grinned. 'But there are some things you wish they'd leave at home?'

'Precisely.'

'As you've just said . . . things are changing.'

General Chandler sighed. 'My children have always thrown my words back at me.'

'It's tough being a pop, Pop.'

The general gave up with a smile of resignation and went upstairs to see his sick wife.

Susan looked at her brother. 'So where's this place they're sending you to?'

'Way up north somewhere. God knows what it will be like.'

'Can't you tell me more?'

'You know I can't.'

'But you will write?'

'As much as the censors will allow.'

'Mother would appreciate it. She'd like to know you're safe. I'd like to know you're safe.'

'I'll try to keep in touch as much as I can.'

'Please do.'

She gave a sigh that was full of both frustration and resignation. 'I do feel I should be doing my bit. I'm young, healthy, strong, single . . .'

'The old boy's right, Suze. Mother needs you here, *and* you can catch up on your studies.'

'I suppose you're right,' she said reluctanctly.

The large, eight-bedroomed country house in the

Malvern hills had been in the family for several generations. The surrounding acreage had already been turned over to the authorities for the duration, for use in food production. A small section of land had been left for the Chandlers' own use, allowing them to be self-sufficient. It was worked by the general's former batman, who also doubled as an unofficial retainer.

The man's life had once been saved by the general in Africa. He had no immediate family and as far as Tim Chandler and his sister were concerned, was simply known as Donald. They had always looked upon him as an uncle, rather than as their father's former personal servant.

Chandler and Susan were in one of the reception rooms and he looked about it, as if seeing the place for the very first time. A glance out of a window showed him the Malverns, dressed in a white capping of snow.

Nothing compared to where I'm going, he thought.

But the rural scene was so peaceful that it seemed at variance with his own presence, an interloping warrior bringing with him the whiff of battles already fought, and of those to come.

'This is what it's all about,' he told Susan softly. 'This is what we're fighting to keep. Imagine some Jerry general commandeering our home to make it his personal billet.'

Susan gave an involuntary shiver. 'I couldn't.'

'Don't worry,' Chandler said, speaking almost to himself and looking out at the hills once more. 'We won't let them set foot in our country – unless it's to die.'

Tim Chandler was twenty-one.

The Hurricanes of Johnstone and Shilling roared low over the airfield, in tight formation. The ground crew were watching. Creddon had brought the car to Dispersal to await the landing.

'Well, he's back,' Clark said unenthusiastically. 'Let's see if he can land.'

Creddon looked at him. 'Won't give up, will you, Nobby?'

Clark looked stubborn. 'I'll do my job, but no one can make me like him. There's nothing in regulations says I have to.'

Creddon shook his head pityingly, then continued, 'Look at that formation. I've never seen one so tight. He's bloody good. Admit it.'

'I don't have to . . .'

But Clark stopped talking as the lead aircraft peeled off and executed a slow roll.

'He's got a kill!' someone shouted. 'Mr Johnstone's got a kill!'

Then there was a sudden hush as Shilling's aircraft also performed a slow roll.

'Bloody hell!' Clark uttered softly. '*He's* bloody got a kill too. First ruddy time out!'

Creddon was grinning. 'Put *that* in your pipe and smoke it, Nobby bloody Clark!'

'The CO and Mr Peters got nothing,' someone else said. 'This won't please them.'

Won't please the CO, you mean, Creddon thought.

Both aircraft made perfect landings.

'He can land, Nobby,' Creddon said mildly.

'Ah, shut up!'

Creddon smiled and walked back to the car to wait.

The Hurricanes taxied to Dispersal and stopped next to each other. The throaty roar of the Merlins died as the pilots cut their power.

Johnstone was the first out, virtually leaping out of his aircraft to rush over to Shilling's. He climbed on to the wing root and up to the hump-backed cockpit, just as Shilling began to release his harness.

'Well done, young Bob!' Johnstone enthused. 'I saw part of your attack on that 88. By God! You were fast into him. I thought you were going to ram the wretched Hun, you got so close!' He peered into the cockpit. 'Kept your lunch too, I see.'

Shilling took a few deep breaths as if ensuring

himself he was still alive, then gave Johnstone a hesitant grin. 'Yes, sir. As for those Jerries, I didn't want to give them time to think. I was worried about those guns getting a bead on me.'

'You certainly didn't give them any time to do that. A celebration in the mess is definitely called for. I'll organize it!'

Their ground crew were now standing about the aircraft. The flight sergeant had also appeared.

'Flight,' Johnstone called down, 'a bright new swastika beneath the cockpit for young Bob. Got himself a fat, meaty Ju-88. One pass and bingo . . . goodbye 88. And find Brandon. I want him to paint a nice round shilling on B for Baker's tail. From now on, this is young Bob's aircraft.'

'Yes, sir,' said the flight sergeant. 'How big should the shilling be, sir?'

'So we can all see it. Tell Brandon to use his imagination. He's the artist, isn't he? Oh yes . . . pop another swastika up for me. Bagged a 109.'

'Yes, sir.'

'Come on, old son,' Johnstone continued to Shilling. 'Out of there. Let's get you to debriefing, then it's on to the mess. Meet the rest of the boys.' He looked up. 'In fact, some of them are coming at this moment.'

As Shilling began to climb out, the flight sergeant said to Johnstone, 'The CO's back, sir.'

Johnstone climbed down off the Hurricane's wing. 'Both back OK?'

'Yes, sir.'

'Good. Any kills?'

The flight sergeant shook his head slowly.

'Luck of the draw,' Johnstone said. He glanced back. 'Come on, young man. Leave that aeroplane alone. You'll be back in there soon enough.'

Shilling came down the wing and dropped to the ground, aware that the ground crew were all staring at him.

'Congratulations, Sergeant,' the flight sergeant said to him neutrally.

'Thank you, Flight.'

They continued to watch him as he followed Johnstone to where Creddon was waiting with the car.

A pair of Hurricanes roared into the air just as they reached it. A few of the squadron pilots had by then arrived and they stared at Shilling with a sharp curiosity that made him feel as if he were some rare specimen in a zoo.

'Gentlemen!' Johnstone began expansively. 'Let me introduce our newest recruit, Sergeant Jack "Bob" Shilling. I took him up for the usual check and I couldn't lose him! *And* he's come back a fully blooded warrior. Flamed an 88 all by himself.'

They continued to stare at Shilling with a mixture of awe and disbelief.

'Young Bob, these reprobates are Paul Chivers – we call him "Jam" – Tom Harris, "Tweed", of course; Henry "Hank the Yank" Sample, from deepest Surrey – never been to America in his life – and James "the Bank" Ellerton. He really did work in a bank. You'll meet the others later.'

Although the assembled pilots were all officers, Johnstone had chosen not to introduce them by rank.

'Come on, gentlemen!' he urged. 'Shake the man by the hand!'

They each did so, offering Shilling congratulations; but there was no real warmth in it.

'Away to the mess hut, you lot,' Johnstone went on. 'Young Bob and I are first off to debriefing, then we'll join you. He's coming as my guest. All right, Two-Wheel,' he added to Creddon as the others departed. 'We're ready.'

'Sir,' Creddon acknowledged. 'Good on you, Sarge,' he said to Shilling, with genuine warmth.

'Thanks, Two-Wheel.'

'*No,*' du Toit said. 'I won't hear of it.'

Johnstone stared at him disbelievingly. 'We *always* celebrate a kill.'

108

'There's nothing to stop you celebrating your kill.'

'And Bob Shilling's?'

'He can celebrate that too . . . in the sergeants' mess.'

'Paul, you can't mean this. How can he celebrate on his own? He's one of our pilots! The lad's just got a kill on his first time out and he should be sharing the event with the others. You can't treat him like that. He's good . . . *better* than good. In fact, he's excellent. Those instructors were right about him.

'He's instinctive,' Johnstone went on enthusiastically, 'as any aspiring, successful fighter pilot ought to be. I did the usual tough formation exercises and he was right there with me. Never once did he fly raggedly. Most people I've taken up lose it after the first few manoeuvres. None of the other pilots currently on the squadron have ever made it through to the end. But the most telling thing of all is that he would have got me, had I been a Jerry.

'When I broke away to practise the attack on him, he behaved completely unexpectedly. Paul . . . that boy has genius. In my opinion he's the best pilot on the squadron. I include myself when I say that. He was on my tail so fast it left me speechless for a moment and he hung on like a leech when I tried to shake him off. The way he dispatched that 88 was a wonder to behold . . .'

'Are you quite finished with your eulogy?' du Toit interrupted, not at all happy that in his praise of Shilling's prowess Johnstone had also unwittingly classed the sergeant above him, the squadron commander.

'Paul . . .'

'It seems as if I shall have to remind you, *Flight Lieutenant* Johnstone, as I've been forced to with Michaels, that *I* am in command of this squadron. Unless, of course, you wish to take it up with the station commander.'

Johnstone looked at him, amazed that du Toit was prepared to take matters that far.

'Do you have proof that Shilling actually destroyed that Ju-88?' du Toit said.

'I *saw* the attack . . .'

'You saw the *beginning*, but according to your own debrief, you were soon occupied with the Messerschmitts.'

'That 88 was diving rather steeply, out of control . . .'

'You can't be sure. It was probably heading as quickly as it could for cloud cover. It's a favourite trick.'

'Shilling saw a parachute.'

'But did *you*?'

'I . . .' Johnstone began, but was interrupted by a knock at the door.

'In!' du Toit snapped.

Michaels ambled in with a sheet of paper upon which he'd written some notes.

'Thought you might like to know, sir,' he began mildly, and began to read from the notes. 'Word from the Navy. They picked up four Jerry bodies and one wounded, barely alive. A Messerschmitt 109 went straight in, and a Junkers Ju-88, in several pieces.' He looked up at du Toit. 'Kills are confirmed.'

Du Toit breathed in deeply. 'Thank you.'

'Sir,' said Michaels, then, after an impassive glance at Johnstone, turned and left the room.

Du Toit's pale eyes turned on Johnstone. 'Shilling will have to delay his celebration. Can't have one of my pilots drinking before he flies.'

'Before . . . Paul, don't . . .'

'Sergeant Shilling will be my number two on the afternoon patrol. Who knows? We might spot another Ju-88. Then I shall be able to see for myself how your paragon performs in combat.'

'*Paul* . . .'

'Thank you, Flight Lieutenant Johnstone. That will be all.'

'Sir.'

Johnstone just managed to keep his fury in check as he strode out of the room.

* * *

A bemused Shilling walked towards his refuelled and rearmed Hurricane. Creddon had brought him word that the CO wanted him at Dispersal, ready for take-off on patrol. He found Johnstone waiting.

'Unexpected change of plan,' Johnstone began apologetically. 'Watch yourself up there, young Bob.'

'Yes, sir.'

Johnstone looked at the new artwork on the aircraft. A neat swastika adorned the cockpit rim, and on the forward section of the tail, high on the fin, was a perfect rendition of a shilling, about the size of a dessert plate.

'Brandon's done you proud,' Johnstone said. 'Excellent work. From now on, when I spot that shilling in the air I'll know who's terrorizing the enemy.' He clapped Shilling on the shoulder. 'The CO's on his way. We'll have our celebration when you get back.'

'Yes, sir. Thank you, sir.'

'Thank me later, when you're back down.'

Shilling watched as the officer walked away without a backwards glance, apparently deep in thought. Then the car drew up with Creddon at the wheel, and du Toit got out.

The squadron commander strode purposefully up to the waiting sergeant and scrutinized him coldly.

There was no welcoming smile, despite the fact this was the first time they had met.

'Sergeant Shilling,' du Toit began, 'I'll come straight to the point. I didn't ask for you, and I didn't expect you. Just obey my orders and we'll get on fine until your posting comes through. Is that clear?'

Stunned by this bluntness, Shilling could only say, 'Yes . . . yes, sir!'

Du Toit pointedly ignored Shilling's discomfort and studied the Hurricane's new decoration. His eyes fastened on the design on the tail.

'Who gave you the authority to deface one of His Majesty's aircraft? You believe that because you have managed one kill, you're suddenly an ace?' The pale eyes glared at Shilling. 'Well, Sergeant? What have you to say?'

Shilling remained silent.

'I won't tolerate dumb insolence, Sergeant! *Who gave you the authority?*'

'It was Flight Lieutenant Johnstone's suggestion, sir,' a new voice replied.

Du Toit whirled to face the flight sergeant, who had turned up to check for any last-minute snags.

'Are you his spokesman, Flight?' du Toit snapped.

'No, sir!'

Du Toit glared at them both. 'I want it removed when we return. Is that clear?'

'Yes, sir,' both SNCOs acknowledged in unison.

'All right, Sergeant,' du Toit went on to Shilling. 'Get aboard your aircraft.'

Shilling climbed back into the cockpit he'd vacated not so long before.

Johnstone had received the news about the design on B-Baker's tail, inevitably relayed to him by Creddon. He'd summoned Brandon. Now they stood together, watching as Shilling and du Toit took off.

'How difficult will it be to remove, Brandon?' Johnstone asked, watching as the aircraft climbed away with Shilling's Hurricane characteristically tucked in tightly to du Toit's.

'Not too difficult, sir,' the airman replied. 'Shame, though.'

'Yes, indeed. Can you make it . . . difficult?'

The airman stared at his superior. 'I don't quite follow, sir . . .'

'Suppose the paint left traces so that, short of re-skinning the entire tail, there was no possibility of removing that shilling completely.'

'What you mean, sir, is that there could be a sort of . . . ghostly image left on the tail, almost invisible, but still there . . .' Brandon had spoken straight-faced.

'That's the sort of idea.'

'I could also use a mix of paint that would make it seem to become more visible in bright light, but would normally be a little hard to spot.'

'That's the stuff. And if you're asked about it?'

'It can't be removed completely without a full re-skinning job, sir.'

'I see. Shame, that. Thank you, Brandon.'

'Sir.'

The Hurricanes had disappeared into cloud.

They had been flying for about half an hour above the constant cloud cover, still in tight formation. Du Toit had not spoken in all that time and Shilling had simply concentrated on keeping station, and scanning the sky about him. They had spotted no other aircraft.

Shilling wondered when du Toit would decide to turn for home.

Another fifteen minutes went by with nothing to mar the whiteness of the clouds, for as far as he could see. Du Toit initiated various changes of heading, but their part of sky remained stubbornly empty of enemy aircraft.

Shilling was looking to his left when a distant speck caught his eye. He checked again just to make certain. A bad call would only make the irate du Toit even more so.

There were *two* shapes cruising above the tufted cloudscape.

Too big at that distance to be fighters. That eliminated the possibility of Hurricanes or Spitfires. They were Ju-88s – he was sure of it – and flying in company for mutual protection. Was that because they had ventured out without escorts?

'*Bandits, bandits!*' he called. 'Eight o'clock. Low!'

'All right, all right,' du Toit responded. 'I see them. Keep your shirt on. Follow me.'

Shilling followed his squadron commander into a tight turn to port before accelerating towards the enemy aircraft, and going into a wide right turn to bring them in for a stern attack.

Shilling did not like that idea. Two 88s meant *four* rearward-firing guns to take concentrated interest in them. The attack should be split, forcing the gunners to hunt for a target.

He did not voice his unease but instead stayed close to his commander as they hurtled towards the enemy bombers. All the while he kept a good lookout for escorts. It was quite possible, as he'd first assumed, that the 88s were tucked in together for mutual protection and were really without escort. It was also possible they were hoping they could sneak in on an anti-shipping strike by initially hiding above the cloud, ready to plunge into it for safety, if spotted. On the other hand, it was equally entirely possible that a gaggle of Me-109s were lurking up top, ready to pounce on any RAF fighters that raced in towards what seemed like relatively easy meat.

So far, he could see nothing but the two 88s.

'Line astern!' came du Toit's terse order.

Another error, Shilling felt, as he obediently took up station to trail behind his leader. He'd still hoped that du Toit, in the end, would have chosen to carry out the attack from separate points, forcing the 88s' gunners to divide their attention. As it was, all the gunners had to do was wait for the two fighters to line up nicely, like a pair of ducks coming in for the privilege of getting shot.

The 88s still appeared not to have spotted the two Hurricanes, for they kept their rigid formation and did not alter heading, looking for all the world as if on a sightseeing cruise.

Or were they the bait for a nicely sprung trap?

Shilling did another rapid scan. Nothing. It seemed there really were just the two Hurricanes and the two 88s in this patch of sky. He hoped.

He allowed his mind to snap back to something the squadron leader instructor with the burnt face had said to him.

'Remember the three Ks,' the squadron leader had advised. 'Kill the pilot, kill the gunners, kill the engines – in any order. One or more will give you a significant advantage. Of course, if you get the pilot, you've won. Never attack a Ju-88 within reach of the guns if you can possibly help it. My favoured method is the beam attack, or the head-on from slightly above.

'The beam attack gives you the best option. The nose gun can be discounted, as can the ventral gun, blanked as it will be by the body of the aircraft. The top gunner is also restricted. Your best approach is diagonally from slightly to the front and above. March your strikes across the airframe. You'll have several hits that way. You should get an engine, which immediately cripples the target. If lucky, you might get both engines. For good measure you might also get both the pilot and the top gunner. If that happens, it is, of course, curtains for the target.'

But that had been another squadron leader. This one was carrying the attack into the teeth of the guns. Shilling wished he'd been flying with Johnstone in the lead. Johnstone would have given him more autonomy. But du Toit was his squadron commander, and he was the sergeant.

He watched helplessly as du Toit dived into the attack. The gunners seemed to have belatedly woken; but they made up for their tardiness by laying down a lethal cone of concentrated fire. Du Toit seemed to fly directly into it.

Shilling could scarcely believe it when du Toit's Hurricane went through that fire and continued to fly. The aircraft seemed unscathed. If du Toit had a guardian angel, he was working overtime. But the fierce defensive fire must have unnerved du Toit, for the 88s flew steadily on, apparently determined not to break formation and thus halve the effectiveness of their guns. His Hurricane had dived away and was swinging round for another pass.

'Get in there, Sergeant!' came the South African's harsh voice.

Shilling attacked in a zigzag pattern, forcing the gunners to try to follow him. It disrupted their cone of fire, which began to disperse raggedly. He fired economically as he dived through, then pulled into a climb just as du Toit began a second pass. In the bright sun above the cloud bank, Brandon's cleverly executed design on the tail of B-Baker gleamed momentarily.

Shilling wasn't certain he'd scored any hits, but as he pulled over the top and looked through the canopy, he thought he saw smoke coming from one of the 88s below him. His strikes? Or du Toit's?

He had positioned himself so that he would be approaching the enemy aircraft from the beam. If du Toit questioned him about that afterwards, he would say his avoidance manoeuvre had placed him there.

As he completed the loop and was again approaching the 88s, he saw that one was indeed trailing heavy smoke; but the formation had remained intact.

Du Toit had completed his second pass and now Shilling had found himself nicely positioned for the classic beam attack that his old instructor had told him about. He fired at the nearest 88 and watched his cannon strikes march along the right wing just outboard of the right engine, strike the engine, cross over to the cockpit then tear across the inner left wing and into the left engine as he rocketed past.

He pulled up into another climb but instead of continuing into the loop, banked punishingly left to come tightly round so as to continue the attack from the port beam. He need not have bothered. The aircraft had disappeared. He jinked once, twice, to search for it. It was heading for the clouds in a perpendicular dive, trailing smoke and flame.

So was the second 88. But this one was still intact. It was heading for the clouds in a desperate quest for safety. Du Toit was plunging after it. Shilling followed.

All three aircraft entered cloud. Shilling altered his heading slightly so as not to run too close to either aeroplane as the whiteness enveloped him in a surreal world where even the racing Merlin took on a muted roar. Insubstantial tufts whirled about the Hurricane. Intermittently, he observed vague shapes ahead of him.

Then he was suddenly out of cloud and the cold, bleak sea was rushing up at him.

The 88 pulled out so low that it appeared to be skimming the surface. Du Toit's Hurricane was right on its tail, with Shilling not far behind. The formation flashed across a ship that seemed to have appeared out of nowhere. Mercifully, it did not fire at them.

Then Shilling saw flashes coming from du Toit's Hurricane before it pulled into a steep climb, breaking off the attack. Shilling pressed on. There was no fire coming from the guns. Had du Toit succeeded in killing the gunners? But there was no smoke from the enemy bomber either, to signify a seriously wounding hit.

Shilling drew closer until the aircraft seemed to fill his world. He fired.

The four cannon thudded murderously as shells tore into the 88, giving off sharp flashes as they struck. The aircraft flew on, seemingly untouched, until suddenly it erupted in a searing ball of flame, forcing Shilling to take violent evasive action to escape flying debris.

He curved round low over the sea, then climbed

in search of du Toit. His squadron commander was just below the cloud base, about a mile to his right.

'Join up, Sergeant!' came the order.

Shilling accelerated towards the other Hurricane and slotted into position. They headed home at low level, in silence.

They landed in near darkness. When he had climbed out of his aircraft, Shilling found du Toit waiting for him a short distance away.

'You did not follow my instructions!' du Toit began accusingly. 'You attacked from the beam!'

'Only because my avoidance of the guns placed me there, sir,' Shilling explained.

Du Toit said nothing to that for some moments, content to stare at Shilling in the gloom.

'I expect you to confirm my two kills,' du Toit said at last.

Shilling felt his mouth open in astonishment. He had expected that they would have claimed a half-kill on the two 88s, thus in effect giving them a whole kill each. He did not argue.

'Yes, sir,' he said.

'Good.'

The flight sergeant crew chief emerged out of the increasing darkness as the ground crew swarmed over the returned aircraft.

'Any luck, sir?' the flight sergeant asked.

'I got two Ju-88s,' du Toit replied. 'Sergeant Shilling will confirm.'

Shilling felt the flight sergeant looking in his direction. 'Two kills,' he said.

He could not properly read the flight sergeant's expression without peering at him, but knew the other was studying him keenly.

'And I want that unauthorized marking removed from the tail of your aircraft,' du Toit said as a parting shot to Shilling.

'Yes, sir.'

As always, Creddon was waiting with the car. Du Toit went over to it and climbed in. The car started off, leaving Shilling to make his way on foot.

Shilling was in his sleeping quarters when Johnstone appeared at the door. The officer was carrying two bottles of beer.

'I can only come in if I'm invited,' he said as Shilling began to get to his feet and was motioned back down.

'You're invited, sir.'

'I accept the invitation,' Johnstone said, and entered.

He put the beers down on one of the bedside lockers, and sat down on the unused bed. With some reverence, he fished an opener out of a breast pocket, and opened both bottles. He passed one to Shilling.

'We can do this out of the bottle, can't we?'

'Yes, sir.'

'Let's dispense with formality for the moment, young Bob,' Johnstone said. He raised his bottle. 'Here's to your continuing health, and to your kills. Sorry we're not doing this in the mess.'

Shilling took a mouthful of beer, then paused. 'I've had *one* kill today.'

'I think not,' Johnstone said. 'You got those kills on those 88s, didn't you?'

'No. The CO did.'

'Is that your last word on the matter?'

Shilling nodded. 'Yes.'

'I see. Well. We'll say no more about it for the moment, but this has not ended as far as I'm concerned.'

6

One of the ferocious storms that Shilling had been warned about by Creddon was approaching Fort Town. All the aircraft – except for two – were safely hangared as soon as it became obvious that severe weather was about to hit the station. Against Johnstone's advice, du Toit decided to mount a patrol, despite the fact that the Navy had informed the unit to expect at least two days of exceptionally high winds.

'The patrol *will* take off,' du Toit insisted to Johnstone. 'The Ju-88s have a habit of using bad weather as cover for anti-shipping strikes. They expect defending fighters to be grounded and will be surprised by a patrol. I have decided that Sergeant Shilling and Pilot Officer Snaith are to fly the mission.'

Johnstone stared at him. 'They'll never get off the ground.'

'Snaith is a good pilot, and if Shilling is as good

as you think, *he* won't have any trouble, will he? I'll grant you there's a strong breeze out there, but not a storm. Any competent pilot should be able to handle it. I'm not going to have an argument about this, Johnstone.'

Johnstone left du Toit's office in frustration and went to the control tower to watch the take-off.

As leader, Snaith would be the first to commence his run, and through his binoculars Johnstone studied the two aircraft anxiously. Although the storm proper had not yet hit, the winds were strong enough to rock the two Hurricanes at the take-off point. To make matters worse, snow flurries, made horizontal by the wind, had virtually obscured visibility.

Johnstone focused on Shilling's aircraft, shifting to the tail where Brandon's new 'invisible' artwork now reposed. A furious du Toit had reluctantly accepted the explanation for its survival. Even he had balked at the thought of putting a fully serviceable aircraft out of commission for a totally unnecessary re-skin. However, the situation had merely served to make his temper worse. The squadron commander felt cheated, and that he had lost the argument.

Johnstone switched his attention back to Snaith as the lead aircraft began its take-off run. He watched in horror as the Hurricane reached take-off speed, swung violently and was tipped on to a wing by a sudden change of direction in the wind that was now streaking across the runway. Before his appalled eyes the wingtip touched and in an instant the aircraft was pinwheeling along the runway, streaming a huge tail of burning fuel before exploding in a fiery ball that continued to roll in the direction of take-off.

Snaith never had a chance.

Then Johnstone saw that Shilling, after a moment's hesitation, was about to try for his own take-off. Johnstone grabbed a microphone from one of the controllers.

'B-Baker, abort! Repeat . . . abort!'

He waited tensely until he heard Shilling's calm acknowledgement.

'Roger. Aborting.'

The Hurricane gingerly turned off the runway and began taxiing back, as the fire-fighting teams and a redundant ambulance raced towards the crash.

Johnstone handed the mike back to the shocked controller and stumped out of the tower to head back to du Toit's office. A silent Creddon was waiting with the car outside the tower, in the increasingly stormy conditions.

As soon as they arrived at the squadron hut, Johnstone barged in without knocking.

'Happy now?' he shouted at the South African.

'Any competent pilot should have been able to take off, should he? Could you have done it? I've scrubbed the mission.' He waited, eagerly hoping du Toit would object, so he could give full vent to the anger he felt.

But du Toit, who'd heard the terrible sound of the explosion even above the noise of the approaching storm, looked pale. Yet he did not back down.

'This is wartime!' he snapped in response. 'These things happen in a war. Do you think bad weather prevents the Navy from putting to sea? Do you think the Condors and the Ju-88s won't be flying their anti-shipping strikes?'

'Well, Snaith won't be flying any more, *will he?* What will you write to his parents? "Dear Mr and Mrs Snaith. Your son died bravely in a ball of fire at the end of the runway because I was too *stupid* to cancel a mission in severe weather." *Is that what you'll say?*'

'You watch your tone when you speak to me, Flight Lieutenant Johnstone!'

'*Or what?* You'll have me court-martialled? How will you explain the reasons?'

'Don't push me, Johnstone! You're not fire-proof!'

'Yes, *sir*!' Johnstone said, saluted mockingly and marched out.

On his way out he nearly collided with Michaels,

who silently invited him into the adjutant's office. Michaels closed the door quietly and handed Johnstone a sheet of paper he'd picked up off his desk.

'It will all end in tears,' Michaels observed portentously.

'Not because I want it to,' Johnstone said.

Regaining his composure, he studied the sheet of paper. It was another confirmation of a kill, from the Navy. The circumstances were very detailed.

The ship that Shilling and du Toit had flown over in pursuit of the sea-skimming Ju-88 had watched the entire combat, and was thus able to make a very accurate report of the incident. Johnstone read it completely before handing it back.

'According to this,' he said to Michaels, 'one Hurricane broke off the attack without any appreciable damage being observed. But it was the aircraft with the shilling on its tail that pressed home, and destroyed the bomber. As I'd thought in the first place, it was Bob's kill. I'll lay you any bet you'd care to take that he got the other 88, or at least crippled it. Bloody du Toit's robbed him!'

'Even taking into account his . . . um . . . national history,' Michaels began thoughtfully, 'I can't understand why the CO's allowing Shilling's presence to get to him this way. He is, after all, the commanding officer. He's not supposed to display his antipathy so openly. As I've said, it'll all end in tears. And ... I can feel a drink coming on. Medicinal, of course.' He rubbed at the stump of his missing arm.

'Of course. You'll pickle that liver of yours.'

'Too late, old son. It passed that point long ago. So what do we do about the kills? Do we still record both as the CO's?'

'Leave it to me,' Johnstone said grimly.

Outside, the storm worked itself into a fury.

Further south, in France, there was no storm; at least, not a natural one. Leutnant Zürst was about to discover the true nature of his own commanding officer's vindictiveness.

Zürst marched briskly into Oberstleutnant Steinhausen's office, in answer to a summons to appear.

'Ah, Zürst,' Steinhausen began affably, as if pleased to see the junior officer. 'You'll be glad to know we'll no longer be in each other's hair.' The sarcasm was too palpable to ignore. 'It seems as if they've got a great need for pilots up north.' He did not specify where 'north' was. 'You'll be flying the Messerschmitt Bf-110, on escort duties. Very exciting stuff, I've been told. Should be right up your street. It's goodbye to France, I'm afraid.'

Zürst felt a great dismay descend upon him. He was being sent away from France! Worse, he was being taken from single-seaters and dumped into a two-seat, twin-engined fighter. True, the 110 had been designed both as a day and night-fighter, but it was no 109. Not by a long shot.

He saw the smirk on Steinhausen's lips, and knew that his erstwhile commanding officer had worked this through a personal network of cronies.

As if to confirm this suspicion, Steinhausen said, 'Your new commanding officer is an old friend. He'll ensure that your time is well occupied. Don't try to pull any stunts with him. That is all, Zürst. Good luck.'

'*Herr Oberstleutnant!*' Zürst acknowledged tightly, saluted and marched out.

Steinhausen waved a hand vaguely in response, and watched as the door closed behind the lieutenant.

'Good riddance,' he said, pleased with himself.

At his Norfolk unit Dan Silverdale was in the presence of his CO, a Canadian squadron leader, for much happier reasons.

'Take a pew, Dan,' James Craigie said. 'Coffee?'

'Thank you, sir,' Silverdale said and sat down in one of the opulent brown leather armchairs. By virtue of its clandestine nature, the special unit appeared to live in conditions most others would seriously envy.

Craigie ordered coffee for two by intercom. 'The repercussions from your very successful mission in France,' he went on to Silverdale, 'are still being felt. By the way, there's a bar to your gong for this. My recommendation.'

'Thanks, sir,' Silverdale repeated.

'Don't thank me. You deserve it. What you brought back in that briefcase sent shivers through those who knew how to interpret the material in it. The Germans are going berserk over its loss.

'News is that they're carrying out punitive raids on any village with the slightest suspected connection with the Resistance, and sometimes no suspicion is necessary. They do it anyway. They've also executed the commander of the unit that pursued your Resistance pals. Thing is, the raids on those villages are stoking up a hatred that's going to blow up in their faces one day. But they sure don't care about that right now.'

'Am I allowed to know what was in that case, sir?'

'Even I don't know, Dan. But I can tell you this: some kind of devastating weapon is being designed. Something that only a very few scientists have any idea about. Part of this experimental activity is taking place in occupied Norway. What was in the briefcase ties in with that.

'Another piece to the puzzle is to be brought out

from Norway, by a Norwegian agent. The plan is to pick him up when he's ready to get out. A Lysander, temporarily based in the north of Scotland, will be tasked to do the job.

'It has been decided that sending the Lizzie to Scotland will muddy the scent for any enemy intelligence people or recce aircraft that may come our way. The northern unit is a pure fighter station, so a clandestine mission from there will not be suspected. As yet, no pilot has been given the mission. Timing is still fluid. I thought I would offer it to you first. You do not have to accept.'

'Of course I'll do it, sir.'

Craigie looked at Silverdale for some moments. 'I won't waste your time and mine by impressing upon you the dangers inherent in this mission. The Jerries will be on the alert at every point where this weapon experimentation is taking place. They will expect some kind of further action from us.

'The problem for them is that they have no idea where or when, and so can't take extra special precautions at any particular site. Their other problem is that they would not like to give away the locations of these sites through any undue and observable activity. They know we'll be on the lookout for such added excitements.'

Craigie paused as a middle-aged civilian woman brought in the coffees.

'Thank you, Mrs Ålstrom,' he said, taking the mugs from her. 'Mrs Ålstrom is Norwegian, Dan. She'll brief you on the local area for the landing. This is to be our pilot,' he added to her.

Silverdale got to his feet. 'Mrs . . .'

'Please,' she said. 'Call me Helle. I have been trying with Mr Craigie, but he always refuses.'

'Then you must call me Dan.'

'OK, Dan.

'And I'll do a trade,' Craigie said easily as he handed a mug to Silverdale. 'Call me James, and I'll call you Helle. How about that?'

'OK, Mr . . .' She smiled sheepishly. '. . . James. Now I will leave you to continue.'

As she left, Craigie said, 'You've just seen a scientist.'

'*What?* And she *makes* the coffee?'

'She didn't make it. She brought it in. I wanted you two to meet.'

Silverdale gave his commanding officer an amused look. 'You knew I'd accept, sir.'

'I know my pilots. Helle Ålstrom came to us after we took Narvik,' Craigie went on. 'A success that lasted for a whole two weeks,' he added grimly. 'The story she had to tell gave enough people nightmares to galvanize them into setting up these missions.

'These experiments, whatever they are, have something to do with water. Only the boffins know what this connection with water has to do with the weapon. However, it seems fairly certain that major operations will be mounted in the future against the locations dealing with it. It is therefore most important that your part in this proves successful. That agent must get back here alive and able to deliver his information.'

'I'll make sure of it, sir.'

'I know you will, Dan. By the way,' Craigie continued in a lighter tone of voice, 'a strange message has come out of France. It was sent to "the pilot who made me push his aeroplane. Tommy is working very well." Make any sense to you?'

Silverdale grinned. 'Yes, sir.'

The day after the storms dawned in pristine beauty. A fresh layer of snow cloaked the surrounding countryside, but there was none on the runways, which had been cleared at first light. It was a bright, still day. The coastal waters were remarkably calm, and the sky was cloudless. It was as if the stormy violence of the past two days had been an act of cleansing. Nature had cleansed itself while humanity continued its orgy of fratricide.

Johnstone was walking his way to Dispersal when the sound of a Hurricane revving up for take-off made him pause to look. It was B-Baker, Shilling's aircraft.

Johnstone smiled. Young Bob was keen. First flying day after the bad weather and he was going up for an 'air test', the excuse the keener pilots tended to use just to get into the air.

He stopped to watch the take-off. It was, as he'd come to expect of Shilling, a perfect lift-off. Then he frowned. Shilling was not turning within the air-field circuit to carry out a few manoeuvres. Instead the Hurricane continued to climb, heading away from its base.

Johnstone stopped a passing airman. 'That is Sergeant Shilling aloft, isn't it?'

'Er . . . I'm not sure, sir.'

'All right. Carry on.'

'Sir.'

Johnstone went to find the flight sergeant crew chief. He found the senior NCO supervising some work in a hangar.

'Flight,' he began, 'was that Sergeant Shilling in B-Baker?'

The flight sergeant looked surprised. 'I thought you knew, sir.'

Johnstone did not like the sound of that at all. 'Knew what?'

'He's gone on patrol.'

'By *himself*?'

The flight sergeant was now hesitant. 'Well, sir . . . the CO ordered it.'

'He . . .' Johnstone paused, biting back the outburst he felt trying to force itself out of him. 'Thank you, Flight.'

'Sir.' The flight sergeant looked at him warily now. 'Nothing I could do, sir.'

'Not your fault, Flight. Not your fault.'

'Sir.'

Johnstone stormed into du Toit's office.

'Don't you knock any more?' the CO demanded.

'Cut the bull!' Johnstone snapped. 'Are you *insane*? You send out a *single* Hurricane on a day like this? Any Messerschmitts in the area will spot him for miles and think Christmas has come early. They'll chew him to pieces.'

'It's not a full combat patrol,' du Toit said smoothly. 'It's a spotter mission. If he sights an anti-shipping raid, he's to radio base immediately with the co-ordinates, and we'll send a force to the area.'

'The Navy, whose ships they happen to be, can do that, as they've been doing all along.'

But du Toit was not to be deflected. 'You and I both know we don't always get the information in time. That's why we have our patrols, so that we can find the raiders *before* they strike. I'm merely utilizing the forces at my command wisely. We lost one aircraft in the storm . . .'

'Which would not have occurred if you had not ordered a patrol that day . . .'

'We lost one aircraft during the storm,' du Toit repeated firmly, 'and two damaged when one of the hangars suffered a blow-in. I'm also down two pilots now, including Snaith. As you're aware, we're still waiting for the second replacement pilot, who should have arrived about the same time as Shilling.'

Johnstone looked at his superior coldly. 'You want him to die, don't you, you b . . .'

'Don't say anything I may not be able to ignore, and you might have cause to regret – Deputy CO or not. In any case, since you rate Shilling so highly, he'll be able to take care of himself, won't he?'

Johnstone's eyes were hot with anger. 'At least any kill he makes will be his this time.'

Du Toit's eyes seemed to grow even paler. 'What the hell do you mean?'

'Think about it,' Johnstone snarled, and went out.

Shilling flew the Hurricane at 12,000 feet, enjoying the vast expanse of empty sky about him. Now and then he spotted ships below him; but there was no sign of any raiders. The still-looking waters, he knew, would be as cold as ever, and could freeze a man to death in rapid order. He had no wish to find out how long that would take in his case. Even so, it was a truly beautiful day to be admired.

But he was amazed by the lack of air activity, for it was also a good day for an attack. On the other hand, he thought, there was no cloud cover, which would make the Ju-88s very vulnerable indeed. But he had no intention of succumbing to complacency. Any raids today, he felt certain, would be escorted.

He went into a lazy turn. The sky was his playground, and he could almost persuade himself there was no war going on.

He described a series of gentle S-turns, keeping a good lookout all the while. The idyllic day could easily become a deadly one if he allowed his vigilance the slightest lapse. He continually checked the air above, just in case a Messerschmitt or two chose to lurk up there. Nothing. He checked the lower levels.

Then he spotted movement.

It was a fleeting shift of *something*, but he was unsure enough to wipe at the interior of the canopy, just in case a speck of dirt had somehow managed to attach itself to it, and had fooled him into believing he'd seen another aeroplane. He'd heard of pilots going into wild gyrations trying to avoid an attack, only to later discover it was dirt on the windscreen or a fly in the cockpit.

139

But this was neither a fly nor dirt. There were two specks now; then three; then a fourth. The three specks were attacking the fourth. All were at slightly lower altitude.

Three Hurris and an Me-109? Or was it the other way round?

'Baker to base,' he radioed. 'Three aircraft attacking a fourth. Investigating.' He gave the location. 'Have we anything out there?'

'Nothing, Baker,' came the reply.

'Roger. Understood. Out.'

Shilling climbed for more height, then put the Hurricane into a shallow dive and accelerated towards the conflict. He was soon able to distinguish the aircraft. The prey was a single Hurricane, which was magnificently holding its own, but that would not continue for ever. Sooner or later the sheer force of numbers would begin to tell.

Shilling raced towards the whirling aircraft and fell upon a Messerschmitt that was waiting its turn to go into the attack, before the other pilot realized his danger. B-Baker's cannon thundered for two seconds. Forty-four pounds of high explosive struck the 109 in the same spot, ripping off its tail. The rest of the aircraft plunged seawards. The canopy shot outwards and a shape tumbled out. The chute didn't open.

'Thanks!' came a voice on Shilling's earphones

on the emergency channel. 'Evens the odds up a bit.'

'Glad to be of service,' Shilling said. 'Tune to channel Oboe Six. Do you know it?'

'Oboe Six,' the other pilot came back on that channel. 'That answer you?'

The strange Hurricane looked like a standard, eight-machine-gun Mark I.

'Loud and clear,' Shilling replied. 'Now let's rearrange this lot's breakfast.'

'Lead on!'

Now that three-on-one had suddenly become two-on-two, the 109s were not so cocky. Shilling latched on to one that had been lining up for a shot at the previously lone Hurricane, which, now released to fight on more equal terms, promptly engaged the other.

Shilling's target Messerschmitt hurled itself into a dive. He followed, watching the speed build in the Hurricane. He knew what was coming next. The 109 hauled into a steep climb, rocketing upwards, hoping to outdistance the British aircraft. But Shilling's Hurricane was nudging the 400mph mark. Two-handedly he hauled the stick towards him and the nose, slowly, reluctantly at first, began to rise. Then curving upwards, still with plenty of energy, it hurtled after the Messerschmitt.

The enemy pilot must have been astonished to see the Hurricane rearing upwards in his mirror. He flicked away in the climb, heading diagonally back down, using the descent to regain more speed with which to curve round on Shilling's tail.

But Shilling was waiting for that too. As soon as the 109 had flashed past, going downhill, he'd rolled the Hurricane through 140° and pulled hard on the stick. The aircraft seemed to wheel about itself, cutting downwards in an opposite diagonal.

The enemy pilot got his third shock of the day when he saw the Hurricane bearing down on him on a collision course. Self-preservation made him attempt a jink out of the way just as the Hurricane's cannon barked at him briefly.

Eighty 20mm shells landed on the Messerschmitt's cockpit, given added impact by the closing speeds of the two aircraft. The blow disintegrated the 109's cockpit, mincing the pilot in an explosive hell.

Shilling flicked the Hurricane away and down, to escape the flying debris as the 109 exploded above him.

When it was all over, all three Messerschmitts had gone down, the unknown Hurricane pilot having finished off the third.

'What nasty big teeth you've got,' the unknown pilot said, closing formation with Shilling's aircraft. 'You're certainly handy with that thing.'

'I try.'

The other pilot laughed. It was the sound of someone who enjoyed being alive. 'If that's how you are when you're just trying, I'm looking forward to seeing you practise the art when you think you're on form. Can I have some teeth like that?'

'If you ask nicely.'

Another cheerful laugh came over the radio. 'You must come to dinner for saving my bacon, if you'll pardon the atrocious pun.'

'Atrocious pun pardoned. Where?'

'Home, of course.'

'And where's that?'

'All will be revealed. Now tell me, you wouldn't know of an airfield around here, would you? I'm due there.'

'Follow me and find out.'

'Roger. Lead on.'

Shilling came in low across the airfield. He went into two slow rolls, followed by the trailing aircraft's single.

On the ground, Johnstone watched the performance with pleasure, and with great relief that

Shilling was alive. Shilling had radioed ahead to warn he was bringing in an extra aircraft.

'Those two kills will make up for the ones you were robbed of, young Bob,' Johnstone murmured to himself. 'That ought to make du Toit happy.' He grinned with relish as he thought of the CO's reaction.

The Hurricanes landed in formation and taxied to Dispersal. The stranger, two swastikas already on his cockpit rim, was first out of his aircraft and ran over to B-Baker. He climbed up to the cockpit just as Shilling removed his flying helmet. His eyebrows rose in surprise when he saw Shilling, then he grinned and held out a hand. 'Tim Chandler. People who ought to know better call me Shippy. If I were Chinese, I would say my life now belongs to you. As I'm not, a weekend at home to go with that dinner, is offered.'

Shilling liked Chandler, a flying officer, on sight. They shook hands.

'Accepted,' Shilling said.

They grinned at each other, and for the first time since he'd arrived at Fort Town,' Shilling felt his loneliness slipping off him like a too-heavy overcoat.

'If this is Fort Town,' Chandler was saying, 'I'm a replacement.'

'This is Fort Town, and you're very welcome.'

Chandler spotted the swastika beneath the cock-pit rim. 'Two more to be added there.'

'The more the merrier,' Shilling said.

They laughed, and Chandler went back down. Shilling got out and followed. They paused by the tail as Chandler looked up at Brandon's handiwork.

'My word,' he said. 'That looks like a bob.'

'It is. I'm Jack Shilling, called Bob.'

'I like it. Has a sort of ring to it!'

They both laughed again. They saw Johnstone approaching.

'Who's that?' asked Chandler. 'CO?'

'Deputy. Flight Lieutenant Johnstone. Gongs up to his ears. Really good sort.'

'Glad to hear it. And the CO?'

'Ah. Well . . .'

But Johnstone had reached them.

Chandler introduced himself. 'Flying Officer Chandler, sir. Replacement. Nearly wasn't, if it hadn't been for Bob here. Tore into those Jerries like an avenging angel. Me-109s. Two down. Luckily for me, he left me the third.'

Johnstone smiled, and shook Chandler's hand. 'That's our Bob. Welcome to the Fort. We've been expecting you for some time.'

'Sorry about that, sir. I was given a short pass to

see the family. Then I had to wait out the storm at Prestwick.'

'It was a bad one. But you're here in one piece, and that's what matters. Get on to debriefing, gentlemen. Mr Chandler, I'll see you in my office afterwards and introduce you to the CO. Bob will show you where. As for you, Bob, get something to eat. I'll see that your new swastikas are put on; although I'll really be seeing five.'

'Five?' Chandler asked after Johnstone had gone and they moved away from the aircraft, leaving them to the ministrations of the ground crew. 'What did he mean?'

'It's a long story.'

'Mystery! I like mysteries.'

'Not this one, you won't.'

'Curiouser and curiouser. He likes you, the deputy CO.'

'He's been very good and fair to me since I've been here.'

'Hmm. You intrigue me, Bob. I know someone who would be fascinated.'

'Who?'

'My sister, Susan. You'll meet her when you come for the weekend. Bit of a handful at times, but she's OK. You'll like her. Now let's go and tell the resident spy how terribly bold we've been.'

* * *

'Are you by any chance related to a General Chandler?' du Toit asked affably as Chandler entered the office, accompanied by Johnstone.

Chandler came to a respectful halt. 'Yes, sir,' he replied with some surprise. 'He's my father.'

'Stand easy. Glad to have you with us, Tim.' Du Toit rose, smiling, from behind his desk to come forward with extended hand. 'I've had the pleasure of meeting the general – in South Africa. I was a very junior liaison officer then. He probably would not remember me.'

'He probably would, sir,' Chandler said as they shook hands. 'He has a tremendous memory for faces. Donald, his former batman, used to say that ability struck terror into everyone, from officers down.'

Du Toit smiled briefly. 'The joys of command. So you found yourself an unofficial reception committee on the way here?'

'Yes, sir. And if it hadn't been for Sergeant Shilling, I wouldn't have made it at all. Quite a terror in the air, sir. He really tore into those Jerries. Chewed them up like a mincer.'

'Ah yes. Shilling.' Du Toit's voice had become several degrees cooler.

From his vantage-point in a corner, Johnstone watched with interest the sudden change in the squadron commander's demeanour, and wondered what Chandler would make of it.

Then du Toit made a supreme effort and brightened once more. 'Well, Mr Chandler. Get yourself settled in at the mess. Creddon, the squadron driver, will take you there. Got much kit?'

'Only what I could stow in the Hurri, sir. But I managed to get some stowage space on an Anson that's coming up next week. The rest of my kit will be aboard.'

'I see. Very well.' Du Toit paused, then went on, 'Our aircraft are Hurricane IICs, and rather more potent than the Mark I.'

'I know, sir. And having seen it in action, I'm anxious for my first flight.'

'Your chance will come soon enough. Flight Lieutenant Johnstone's in charge of the training programme, and will show you the ropes.' Du Toit chose not to look at Johnstone as he spoke.

'Sir.'

'That is all for now. Do give your father my regards when next you see him.'

'I will, sir. He'll be quite astonished to discover that you are my CO.'

Du Toit's smile was enigmatic. 'The war sometimes creates the strangest of circumstances.'

'It certainly does, sir.'

'Thank you, Mr Chandler.'

'Sir.'

Chandler went out to find Creddon.

Johnstone remained, his eyes fixing du Toit. 'Well, he got his two kills and didn't die, after all.'

'Is that a tone of accusation?'

'Absolutely not,' Johnstone replied, and then went out.

7

Two days later another storm hit the station. This time, though it was not as bad as the previous one, no one was sent aloft on patrol, and no accidents occurred. Du Toit had apparently learned *that* lesson.

The friendship that had sprung up between Shilling and Chandler grew stronger. Chandler had been introduced to the Hurricane IIC by Johnstone and had done one practice sortie, with Shilling in the lead. As Johnstone was in charge of training, there was not much du Toit could have done about that particular pairing.

As the storm howled outside, Shilling, Chandler and Johnstone sat in Shilling's quarters with a beer each.

'Well?' Johnstone began to Chandler. 'How do you like our holiday weather?'

'Is it always as bad?'

'Worse. This is a mild blow, isn't it, young Bob?'

'It certainly is. You should have been here when we lost Snaith, Shippy . . .' the sergeant added to Chandler, then stopped. Shilling raised his bottle. 'To absent ones,' he said quietly.

'To Snaith.'

'Snaith,' the others said together. They all drank a toast to the dead pilot.

'I've got to ask this, Bob,' Chandler said, glancing at Johnstone. 'What's the problem between you and the CO?'

Shilling looked at his bottle and said nothing.

It was Johnstone who partially supplied the answer. 'The CO has some difficulty coming to terms with Bob's . . . er . . . it's all so stupid . . .'

Chandler understood at once. 'You mean his colour?'

Johnstone nodded. 'Crazy, isn't it? Here we are in this frozen world, trying to fend Jerry off and what do we have? A CO prepared to jeopardize the cohesion of his unit because of a personal prejudice.' Johnstone paused, surprised that he'd actually voiced to others the thoughts he'd privately harboured since Shilling's arrival on the unit.

'But the other pilots,' Chandler went on. 'What have they got against Bob?'

'Ah, you see,' Johnstone replied, 'it's rather difficult for them. They're reluctant to get into the CO's bad books, whatever their own personal feelings. He's already given up on me, and now you, my dear Chandler, will turn out to be a great disappointment to him. And you a general's son. Tut, tut. And now I've talked out of turn. I would thank you both not to repeat this.'

The other two nodded.

'Unless you hear to the contrary,' Johnstone went on, 'I'm making your pairing a permanent one. Unless you have an objection, Mr Chandler.'

'None at all.'

'I'm giving Bob the lead.'

'Fine by me,' Chandler said.

'The CO might have other ideas,' Shilling suggested.

'I'm doing this for the good of the unit. I happen to think that the two of you have the makings of an excellent combat team. You proved that quite conclusively when you took on those 109s. I will make the point to the CO. Damn it, I've got some rights to decision making on this unit.' He raised his bottle. 'To the confusion of all enemies.'

'The confusion of all enemies,' Shilling and Chandler said together.

Outside, the wind smashed itself dementedly against the hut.

The wind was still battering away the next day, and the cloud base seemed to be at runway level. Flying continued to be suspended, though a four-aircraft formation waited on stand-by in two hangars, hoping for a break in the weather.

The formation, led by Johnstone, consisted of Shilling, Chandler and a pilot officer named Hardacre. In the event, they never managed to get off the ground.

However, a three-aircraft formation of Ju-88s, having taken off in reasonable weather, used the bad conditions over Britain to carry out an anti-shipping raid that day. They badly damaged a destroyer, but two were in turn seriously damaged by ferocious anti-aircraft fire from the ship's pom-poms.

The third aircraft dropped its bombs harmlessly before scuttling for home. One of the returning 88s crashed into the sea, just short of safety.

That same day, Leutnant Zürst arrived at his new unit.

As he waited to see the unit commander, he looked out of a window at the neat line of twin-engined Bf-110Cs, and felt depressed. These were virtually the most basic version of the twin-finned Messerschmitts, similar to those that had been so decimated by the Spitfires and Hurricanes during the Battle of Britain. Now here he was in this God-forsaken place, assigned to escort duties, nursemaiding Ju-88s.

It was enough to turn the stomach of any self-respecting fighter pilot. He wouldn't have minded where he'd been posted, as long as it was to an Me-109 unit. Steinhausen had indeed got his revenge, the bastard.

A hard-looking sergeant came up to him. '*Herr Leutnant?* The colonel will see you now.'

So Steinhausen's friend was a full colonel. It could only get worse.

It did.

The NCO knocked on the unit commander's door.

'*Hierein!*' came the barked command.

The NCO pushed open the door and stood aside for Zürst to enter, before shutting the door once more.

Zürst took one look at the close-cropped, grey-streaked head and knew his fears were about to be realized.

The colonel chose not to look up for several seconds. When he eventually did so, it was to display the hardest pair of eyes Zürst had ever seen and a tight, bony face marked by a duelling scar.

'So you are Zürst,' Colonel Friedo Pfaffenhof began unencouragingly.

'Yes, *Herr Oberst*!' Zürst stood rigidly to attention. The colonel did not order him to stand easy.

'Well, *Leutnant*, I can tell you that this is no unit

for pampered, single-seater glamour boys. This is a hard-working unit whose job is sinking English shipping, of *any* kind. *Your* job will be to make sure the aircraft you are escorting are not shot down before they have completed their mission.

'*All* crews, Ju-88s and Bf-110s alike, know I expect results. There are no exceptions. See Major Stammheim for your conversion training. You'd better be a fast learner. You won't have the luxury of a long period to get accustomed to the aircraft. There's a 109 unit not far from here, and they are frequently assigned escort duties for my 88s. But you're not going there. Dismissed.'

Zürst saluted and turned to go.

'And Zürst . . .'

He paused, waiting for his new commander to speak.

'I'm keeping my eye on you.'

At Fort Town, the weather did not change for the better for two more days. When eventually it did so it was not like the earlier bright and clear conditions, when even the sound of the engines had taken on a surreal edge, as if the very air had become a sound mirror, filled with invisible crystals that reflected the swirling frequencies off each other.

This day was very different. It felt heavy and doleful. But at least Johnstone was finally able to get his formation aloft. He split it into two pairs, he leading the first, Shilling the second.

They climbed steadily, heading for an intercept point between Scapa Flow and mainland Europe. Johnstone felt certain the Ju-88s would come out to play.

The formation rose above the cloud bank which persisted over the sea. Bright sunshine greeted the Hurricanes, turning the dirty grey of the cloudscape into a gleaming whiteness. On cue, the four aircraft split into two pairs, drifting half a mile apart. There was total radio silence. Before take-off, Johnstone had insisted on it, and it was to be broken only when bandits were sighted.

Led by Johnstone into a wide, sweeping pattern, the formation was half an hour into its patrol without sighting anything. He began to wonder whether he'd gauged wrongly. The 88s, if they came, would not fly below the cloud base until ready to attack, betraying themselves to their intended targets at the last possible moment. They would make their approach in the relative safety above the clouds.

At least, Johnstone thought drily, that was the theory. However . . .

'*B-Bandits, bandits!*' An excited Hardacre was the first to spot them. Unfortunately he forgot to add the all-important direction.

'I've got them!' Shilling announced. 'Nine o'clock.

Low and ... *escorts!* Seven o'clock and coming down – 109s!'

'Take the escorts,' Johnstone ordered. 'We'll handle the bombers.'

'Roger,' Shilling acknowledged.

'Blue Two,' Johnstone continued to Hardacre. 'With me!'

'R-Roger!'

'You heard the man,' Shilling said to Chandler. 'Stay low. I'm going up.'

'Roger,' Chandler acknowledged and went into a wide turn to force the descending Messerschmitts to adjust direction.

At the same time Shilling flicked B-Baker on to its back and into a dive, before hauling the stick towards his stomach. The Hurricane bucked slightly then brought its nose up, powering into the climb. Shilling eased the pressure on the stick as the aircraft shot upwards.

A 109 flashed past, firing as it went. It missed.

'Too eager,' Shilling grunted, banking past 90° in the climb and pulling on the stick once more, then easing off so as not to tighten the turn too much.

He was heading back down in a curving dive. The aircraft that had flashed past was turning, wondering where he'd got to.

'Behind you,' he muttered, and fired.

The four-cannon barrage thumped out for one

second. Shilling saw strikes bounce off the top of the 109's cockpit, then merge into the aircraft's body just behind the canopy.

Nothing happened.

He couldn't believe it. Then suddenly a great bloom of fire appeared, and a wing tumbled towards the clouds. The 109's back then seemed to break as it fell after its lost wing.

Shilling saw no parachute, but he didn't wait to check, for a flash of fire streaked past his own cockpit.

'Watch your tail, Shilling!' he admonished himself. 'Your bloody tail!'

He flung the Hurricane once more on to its back, and pulled on the stick as if going into a panic dive. He half-rolled and pulled again, reversing direction, throttling back to kill speed even more as the nose began to come up, the Hurricane's tendency to go tail-heavy in the dive aiding him. He then rolled through 90°, shoved the throttle forward again and hauled the aircraft into the turn, maintaining at least 300mph. The chasing 109 flashed past above his wingtip. He actually saw its pilot looking at him. Then it was gone.

He broke out of the turn, scanning the sky for Chandler. Chandler was racing towards him, in hot pursuit of a 109. Chandler was all right.

Shilling looked for 'his' 109. It was nowhere to be

seen. He checked for Chandler once more. Chandler was in a shallow dive, still glued to the 109.

Instinct made Shilling look further behind the Hurricane. There. The other Messerschmitt was sneaking up on the occupied Chandler.

'Blue Four!' Shilling called. 'Your tail!'

'Sort him out,' came the calm reply. 'I've got his pal.'

'On my way!'

Shilling hurtled after the pursuing 109 on an intercept course. Its pilot appeared not to have seen him, for the enemy aircraft maintained a steady flight towards Chandler's Hurricane. Within seconds the 109 would be in gun range.

Shilling was still too far out. In desperation, he fired the briefest of bursts. It was a waste of ammunition, but it did the trick. The streaming tracers got the 109 pilot's attention. He jinked reactively, ruining his aim and giving Shilling all the time he need to draw closer and get him straddled nicely in the Hurricane's sights.

At the same instant Shilling and Chandler fired at their respective targets. Shilling watched fascinated as his strikes began at the nose of the enemy aircraft, to march along its entire length, and then the 109 vanished. As he banked the Hurricane to check, he saw the Messerschmitt tumbling away. This time, there was a parachute.

A short distance away, something plunged vertically, trailing a long plume of black smoke that contrasted violently with the white of the cloud bank. Then it disappeared as it entered the cloud. Eerily, the plume continued to cone itself out of the cloud bank, a strange growth that marked the passing of another human being.

Chandler joined up with Shilling. The sky seemed clear of enemy aircraft. Then they saw two specks racing towards them and prepared themselves for further combat. To their great relief, the specks turned into Hurricanes. Johnstone and Hardacre on their way back.

'Everyone all right?' Johnstone enquired as soon as they had all rejoined formation.

Shilling and Chandler confirmed they were OK.

'The two 88s never made it,' Johnson went on, temporarily rescinding the radio silence order. 'You?'

'Three 109s,' Chandler said.

'Good show! A fine crop.'

Suddenly Chandler called sharply, 'Blue Three!'

Shilling looked quickly about him. 'Blue Three. What's up?'

'Seems you caught one, old son. I can see daylight intermittently through your fin.'

Johnstone eased back to check. 'He's right. A neat hole, just below the shilling.'

That second 109 had not missed totally, after all. But in combat a near miss was a no-win. The 109 pilot had paid for it.

That will teach you to keep a sharper eye on your tail, Shilling admonished himself for a second time. It was a mistake that could have put him where the enemy pilot now was.

'Any other damage?' Johnstone was saying. 'Controls all right?'

'Perfect,' Shilling replied. 'No control problems whatsoever, and all instruments reading OK.'

'Fit enough to continue patrol?'

'Fit enough.'

'All right, Blue Flight. Radio silence.'

Though they continued the patrol for another hour, there was no more contact with the enemy. Johnstone turned the formation homewards.

The cloud base was almost on the deck when they arrived back at the airfield. Johnstone forbade any victory rolls in such poor visibility and they came in to land in line astern. Johnstone led, followed by Hardacre, then Shilling and Chandler.

Shilling, mindful that perhaps there might have been another cannon strike from the 109 he could have missed, checked brake pressure and noted with satisfaction that it was well over the minimum of 100lb per square inch. He reduced speed to 120mph, slid back the hood and locked it.

He lowered the undercarriage as the speed dropped and got the green lights. Everything fine in that department. Supercharger control was set to moderate, and the flaps were down. No damage there either. Speed was now down to 95 on approach. No problems.

He landed without drama.

The four aircraft taxied to Dispersal, where the eager ground crew were anxious for news of any kills. There was a loud cheer when Johnstone told them.

Johnstone had got one 88, and shared the second kill with Hardacre. Shilling had his two 109s, and Chandler one.

'Your score's mounting,' Johnstone remarked to Shilling as they all studied the hole in his fin. 'Jerry nearly scored today, though, young Bob. Not getting complacent, are you?'

'No, sir. I was pretty annoyed with myself.'

'*Never* get annoyed in combat,' Johnstone told him quietly but firmly. 'That way lies the fatal mistake that could kill you.'

'Yes, sir.'

'I'd like to think you've learned a valuable lesson today.'

'I have.'

'Good.' Johnstone peered at the hole. 'Very neat. Right under the shilling. What repair can we have in there, Brandon?'

Brandon had come to inspect the damage. 'Easy to patch, sir. I could always place a swastika on that spot, to mark the kill there, if the sergeant likes.'

'The sergeant likes,' Shilling said, 'if the Deputy CO will authorize it.'

'The Deputy CO authorizes it,' Johnstone said.

'Right, sir,' Brandon said. 'I'll get it done.' He grinned at them. 'You're all keeping me busy, sir,' he continued to Johnstone. 'All these swastikas I'm having to put up.'

'Let's hope we can continue to keep you very busy, Brandon.'

'Just what I like to hear, sir. It's good for the squadron.'

Johnstone nodded. 'Thank you, Brandon.

'Sir.'

The four pilots began walking away. A short while later, the squadron car drew up next to them. Creddon was driving. They stopped.

Du Toit got out. 'Any luck?'

'Five down,' Johnstone replied. 'Two 109s to Sergeant Shilling, one to Chandler, an 88 to me and a half share of another between Hardacre and myself.'

'Good score. Congratulations.' Du Toit did not look at Shilling. 'Anyone like a lift?'

'I think we'll walk, sir,' Johnstone said. 'All those hours in the cockpit, you know. We could do with stretching the legs a bit.'

Du Toit looked at him impassively. 'Very well. Carry on.'

The squadron commander got back into the car, and it set off with a low whine of gears.

No one said anything as they continued walking.

Though the weather was not perfect, it was good enough for flying and those conditions persisted for a week. There was also sufficient cloud cover to tempt the Ju-88s out, day or night. But despite constant patrols, no enemy aircraft were sighted. There were no attacks on shipping either. It was as if the recent losses had had a salutary effect on the enemy, forcing him to keep his aircraft grounded.

Johnstone did not believe that for a second.

'They're planning something,' he said to du Toit.

'And what would that be?'

'An attack. Here.'

Du Toit stared at him. 'Don't be ridiculous. That's even further to come than for the shipping strikes.'

'It's still within their range, and they can use drop tanks to give them an extra margin of fuel.'

But du Toit still gave the idea little credence. 'With a full bombload and all that extra fuel they'd be great lumbering, explosive sitting ducks just waiting to be picked off. It would be like being in a fairground.'

'They'll have escorts,' Johnstone insisted. 'Plenty of them. If I commanded that Ju-88 unit, I'd turn my attention to the airfield that's sending up those fighters to chew up my bombers ever time I mounted a shipping strike. I'd make certain those fighters were thoroughly neutralized before returning my attention to the ships. I'd send in a mass formation to pulverize the airfield.'

Du Toit surveyed Johnstone without much enthusiasm. 'But you're not in command of a Ju-88 unit. You don't *know* that's what they're planning.'

'It's what I would do.'

'There are many things we would all do individually. Few would match if we compared notes.'

'You've got my opinion, sir,' Johnstone said, keeping his exasperation in check. 'Do with it what you will. I would suggest we ask the Navy to keep a sharp lookout for unexpected formations heading landwards, and put any Observer Corps units in the general area on the alert.'

'And for how long?'

'As long as it takes. They *will* try an attack. I'm convinced of it. It makes tactical sense. We'd look pretty stupid if our aircraft were caught on the ground.'

'*I'd* look pretty stupid, you mean.'

'I didn't say that, Paul.'

'No,' du Toit agreed. 'You didn't.' But that's what you meant, the tone of his voice made clear.

As he left du Toit's office, Johnstone decided to have a talk with Michaels.

'I need some favours, Mike,' he began to the adjutant.

'Let's hear them, then I'll tell you if I can oblige.'

Johnstone outlined his belief in the possibility of an attack on the airfield.

'Makes operational sense,' Michaels commented. 'Shilling, Chandler and yourself have been too successful of late for that Jerry commander – whoever he is – to stomach. He's got to do something. If I were him, an attack would be high on my agenda. If done with the right amount of surprise, it would be devastating. If not, highly expensive. Paul du Toit is right about one thing: those heavily laden Ju-88s *would* be sitting ducks.'

'Not if there was a swarm of fighters to protect them.'

'That *would* alter the equation somewhat. How would you counter a force like that?'

'I'd go out to meet them, and attack long before

they got here. The fighters would still be carrying their drop tanks and would be compelled to jettison them in order to engage in any kind of manoeuvring combat. Once they'd done that, those that survived would have insufficient fuel to continue the escort with any hope of making it back home. More fighters lost. The remaining bombers would be horribly naked, just asking to be chewed. I'd put up a maximum number of Hurricanes, even the Mark I that Chandler brought with him. I'd even send you aloft, Mike, if you had two good arms.'

Michaels gave a smile that was full of irony. 'A drunken, one-armed pilot. That would be something. For what it's worth,' he continued, 'I agree with you entirely. I'll talk to a few naval contacts on the quiet and get things moving. I'll do the same with the Observer Corps.'

'Thanks. I do appreciate it.'

'You're sailing pretty close to the wind,' Michaels said gravely.

'This could be made to seem as if you're seeking to undermine the CO.'

'I'm trying to save his neck, if he could but see it. If we get hit as badly as I fear, he's finished. I'd rather not be proved right.'

'A stitch in time, and all that. I get the drift. I'll do what I can and yes, I'll keep it unobtrusive.'

Johnstone nodded, and went out.

'*Definitely* end in tears,' Michaels said to himself, and reached for the hip-flask.

The days drifted by, and no warning of an impending attack on the airfield was received. No enemy aircraft was seen lurking near any shipping, despite continuing combat patrols.

This proved to du Toit that Johnstone was wrong.

Conversely, the continuing lull served to heighten Johnstone's certainty that something was brewing.

'I'm beginning to have withdrawal symptoms,' Chandler declared on landing after yet another barren patrol. 'It's been ten days since I last shot at something.'

'You'll be doing it again soon enough,' Shilling told him.

'You're far too calm for one so young.' Chandler sniffed at his armpit. 'That Anson had better get here soon with the rest of my things, or even my Hurri will want to keep away from me.'

'Moan, moan, moan,' Shilling said good-naturedly.

Then they stopped to listen as they heard aircraft engines. The warning sirens had not gone off, but they remained poised by their aircraft, ready to leap back into their cockpits. There was still plenty of fuel, and a full load of ammunition.

Then a single aircraft came into view. It was the Anson.

'Talk of the devil!' Chandler exclaimed as he relaxed once more.

'Your armpits won't be so anti-social from now on,' said Shilling.

Chandler looked worried. 'Were they, really?'

Shilling just grinned at him.

The Anson did not bring Chandler's clothes; but it did bring a stranger. Lieutenant Colonel Hennie Marais, South African Army, young-looking and wearing rows of medal ribbons, demanded to be immediately taken to the squadron commander.

A tall, square-built man with the physique of a boxer but without the battered face, Marais looked like the sort of person you crossed at your peril. He was as blond as du Toit, but his hair was cut more severely, almost resembling everyone's idea of a *junker* German officer.

Creddon obliged by driving him to the squadron hut and handing him over to Johnstone, who ushered him in to see du Toit.

Johnstone was stunned to see du Toit go pale, then leap to his feet.

'Hello, Paul,' Marais began. 'Man, it's good to see you after all these years!' He held out his hand. 'I couldn't believe it when they told me who was in command of this squadron. You have done well.'

Du Toit came round his desk to shake Marais' hand, but his heart didn't seem to be in it.

Then he looked at Johnstone. 'You've met my deputy, Flight Lieutenant Johnstone.'

Marais nodded.

'Thank you, Hamish,' du Toit said.

'Sir,' Johnstone acknowledged and went out, puzzled by du Toit's reaction.

He paused briefly by the closed door, long enough to faintly hear du Toit say, 'What do you want here, Hennie?'

There was no welcome in the voice.

Marais looked at du Toit with a thin smile. 'Paul, man. You're not still holding that grudge? We are old friends.'

'We *were* old friends,' du Toit corrected.

Which was quite true. Du Toit and Marais had grown up together. Their families had frequently entertained each other and the boys had been like brothers. One day, as children will, they went exploring a forbidden room in the du

Toits' home. There was nothing special about the room itself; it was little more than a box-room.

There the boys found an old locked chest that seemed to have been forgotten for generations. Curiosity overcame the fear of punishment and they forced open the lock. What they found inside was a treasure trove of old photographs. Wondering what could have been so special about photographs that had been kept in a locked chest, in a locked room, they had begun to study each photo, laughing at the funny way people used to dress in the old days.

Then they had come upon the photograph that was to alter their relationship for ever.

At first, they had seen nothing particular about it. A group of people with a young black female, obviously a servant. But closer scrutiny had shown that she was not dressed like a servant. In fact, the clothes she wore looked quite smart. It was only after a while it finally dawned upon them that they were looking at a wedding photograph. The young black woman was the bride. The groom was white.

'There's a black in your family!' the young Hennie Marais had exclaimed in a shocked whisper.

'Don't be stupid, man!' du Toit had countered.

'That is not my family. It must be a friend of theirs.'

Then Marais had turned the photo over. There, in a simple hand, had been the legend: 'Wedding of Hendryk and Mary du Toit.'

'*No, no, no, no, no!*' du Toit had cried. 'It's not true!'

'Look, man,' Marais had said. 'Don't worry about it. No one is going to know. I am your friend. Do you think I would tell?'

Marais had been as good as his word. Nothing was said of the skeleton in the du Toit family cupboard.

Until the day came when they both fell for the same girl. By then, they were approaching their twenties. Kirsten Willemsteen's beauty had captivated them both, but her preference was for du Toit.

Marais had become enraged by this. The good friend had suddenly become an enemy.

He gave du Toit an ultimatum. Forget Kirsten, or he would tell her about Mary du Toit. Her family would never countenance her association with someone whose blood line possessed such a terrible mark. Kirsten, a paragon of what was best in South African womanhood, would never see him again. If he kept out of the running, she would at least still remain a friend.

Damning every black person on earth for the curse brought on his family, du Toit had left the field to Marais; something a puzzled and upset Kirsten never understood.

Du Toit joined the South African Air Force soon after, and deliberately lost touch with both Marais and Kirsten. He assumed they'd eventually got married. Now his tormentor was right here in his office.

You'd have thought I'd gone far away enough from them, he thought bitterly.

'I see you have changed your mind about blacks,' Marais said, interrupting du Toit's gloomy thoughts. 'I saw a black pilot by one of the Hurricanes, on the way here.'

The pale eyes, full of the pain of the memory of earlier betrayal, merely looked at Marais.

'So you still hate them,' Marais said softly. 'He was dumped on you. Is that it? And you probably think someone knows your little secret and sent him here to haunt you.'

'Would you be that someone?' du Toit demanded tightly.

Marais gave an enigmatic smile, and shook his head slowly.

'What the devil do you want on my squadron, Hennie?'

'You're wrong about me, you know.'

173

'Like hell I am! Just answer me. What are you doing here?'

'I can see we're not going to bury the past.'

'Did you really expect me to?' The pale eyes seemed to blaze with a cold fire.

Marais looked at his erstwhile friend calmly. 'No. I suppose not. So I'd better get to the official business. An operation is being planned from this station. A Lysander aircraft will be coming up here soon, to deliver someone to Norway, and to bring someone else back. Your squadron is to provide an escort there *and* back. It will be dangerous for your pilots. The escort will probably run into trouble as the Nazis will do everything in their power to stop the Lysander. But that Lysander *must return safely*.'

'Couldn't someone else have brought this information to me?'

'I wanted to do it personally. I wanted to see you.'

'Why?'

Marais hesitated. 'I felt it was right.'

'I don't. Are you involved in this operation?'

Marais nodded. 'In part.'

'If my orders are to work with you, I shall. But I don't have to like it.'

'That's right. You don't. I'll be returning to my unit in the Anson later today. You'll be hearing from us. Now, if it's not too much trouble, perhaps you can arrange a meal for me and the crew in the mess.'

'Of course.'

'Thank you.'

8

Zürst had been put through the training wringer by Stammheim. Every day, every night, hour after hour, he was sent up by the major, sometimes on a solo flight, sometimes with a rear gunner, sometimes without, sometimes with the major himself riding shotgun in another aircraft.

Zürst grappled to come to terms with flying the Messerschmitt Bf-110. After the nimble 109 the aircraft, despite its twin Daimler-Benz DB601A 1200hp engines, still felt like a truck. Sitting in the long, glasshouse cockpit with the rear-facing gunner's seat behind him made him feel exposed.

But gradually he began to get the feel of the aircraft. After a while he started to appreciate its powerful weaponry and its long-range endurance. He couldn't flick it around like the 109, but all he needed to do was get an enemy aircraft in his sights just long enough to let loose with his multiple cannon. Nothing could survive that blow.

When Stammheim thought he was good enough, Zürst was given a surprise. He was assigned one of the brand-new Bf-110Es that had been sent to the unit for evaluation. There were six of them. No other unit had as yet received them in normal squadron service.

This new version had extra power in its uprated engines and an even more formidable weapons fit. It had two 30mm and two 20mm cannon in the nose, plus two more 30mm cannon in a belly pack. It also had a night-fighting capability and infrared sensors.

Sheer hell to an enemy, with all that firepower converging on him, Zürst mused with great satisfaction.

The rear gunner had a twin 7.92mm machine-gun to cover the tail.

With a full load of ammunition and fuel, the 110 would just make it to 340mph; but that didn't compare too badly with a Hurricane. If he played things right, Zürst decided, and entered combat with half fuel and thus much lighter, but leaving himself enough to get home, he could make things very uncomfortable for the British fighters. He was determined to confound Steinhausen, by performing well and scoring victories.

It would be the best way to get his own revenge.

On landing after a particularly good flight in the 110E, Zürst was summoned to Pfaffenhof. He entered the unit commander's office and clicked his heels smartly to attention.

'Ah, Zürst,' the colonel began in far warmer tones than at their first meeting. 'Major Stammheim tells me you are his star pupil. Remarkable. When you first got here I had you down as a bad loser who would be pining for his 109 and giving us all a headache with constant whining. Instead, it seems as if you have taken to the 110.'

'I wouldn't go that far, *Herr Oberst*,' Zürst said, rather boldly, all things considered.

'Wouldn't you?' The bony, duel-scarred face was expressionless.

'What I mean, *Herr Oberst*, is that I have come to understand the aeroplane. I now know its weaknesses, and its strengths. I intend to maximize those strengths in combat.'

Pfaffenhof stared unblinkingly at his subordinate, then reached to his right for a gold cigarette case. He flicked it open, pulled out a cigarette and offered the opened case to Zürst.

Zürst, astonished by the offer, took one.

Pfaffenhof snapped the case shut, lit his cigarette, then extended the lighter for Zürst to light up. He flipped the lid down on the lighter, and took a long pull at the cigarette.

'Relax, *Leutnant*,' he continued, blowing smoke at the ceiling. 'As I was saying, Stammheim reckons you use the 110 like a single-seat fighter, despite its size. If you're as good as he thinks, you'll soon get the chance to put it to the test.

'Recently we have been taking serious casualties from a particular British fighter unit. Our shipping strikes have been broken up each time, and even the 109 unit I told you about when you first got here has been taking some severe losses. I have therefore decided that before the anti-ship missions can be resumed, a massive strike against the airfield is to be launched. The Ju-88s will be escorted by both versions of the 110, with the 109s as top cover.'

'When is this to be, sir?'

'When they least expect it.'

Pfaffenhof blew some more smoke at the ceiling, and looked pleased with himself.

At Fort Town, the snow squadron had another week of bandit-free patrols.

'I swear,' Chandler said at the end of yet another patrol with the guns unfired, 'I'm beginning to wonder what the gun button looks like and . . .' He paused to sniff at his armpit. '. . . as that wretched Anson failed to bring up my clothes . . .'

'You take your showers, don't you?' Shilling said with a straight face.

'I'll have you know, my man, that putting on the same clothes, even after a shower, or having to walk around in stores-supplied spare kit which looks and feels as if it came out of the trenches of the First World War, and happens to be in every size except mine, is no substitute.'

'Are you sure those Anson pilots agreed to take your kit?'

'I swear.'

'They weren't drunk? Or come to that ... *you* weren't drunk?'

'Sober as a judge ...'

'You ought to hear what people back home say about judges. Drunk as a Lord Justice, they say ...'

'That's the colonies for you,' Chandler said. 'I vote,' he went on brightly, 'that we ask the Deputy CO very nicely for some leave ...'

'You mean, while the cat's away?'

Du Toit had been summoned to Norfolk to be fully briefed on the Norwegian operation. No one was sure when he'd be back. A distinct air of liveliness, though cautious, had insinuated itself into the squadron with du Toit's departure. Because everyone knew he *would* be back eventually, no one was going overboard with ecstasy.

'We have been putting in the flying hours,' Chandler pointed out. 'More than most, I'd say.

Just forty-eight hours. Enough to locate my kit and visit the family. Your chance to meet Susan.'

'Oh . . . I don't know . . .'

'Don't be a stick-in-the-mud. You'll really like her.'

'But would she like me? And your parents . . .'

'Would love to have you stay.'

Shilling was hesitant. 'I'm not sure about this . . .'

'I know my family. You don't. I'm telling you, you'll be most welcome.'

'Besides,' Shilling began hopefully, 'I can't see old Hamish letting us go.'

'Leave it to me.'

'That's why I'm worried.'

'Oh ye of little faith,' Chandler said cheerfully.

Hamish Johnstone looked from one man to the other. They had been ushered into his office, and had made their request.

'Gentlemen,' he began at last, 'I do hope you're not thinking I'm a soft touch, in the absence of the CO.'

'No, sir!' Shilling declared, horrified that the Deputy CO would even think it.

'Perish the thought,' Chandler echoed.

Johnstone again studied them silently.

'Gentlemen,' he said at last, 'you'll no doubt have been exercising your minds, trying to equate the increased frequency of our patrols with the patent fact that the enemy appears to have gone on holiday.

'I happen to think that the Hun has not called off the war in this neck of the woods, but is actually in the process of planning something rather nasty for us. I believe he intends to deal this station a knock-out blow, if he possibly can.'

They stared at him.

'I would, in his place,' Johnstone told them calmly.

'We've been hurting him,' Chandler said. 'It makes sense. He can't go after the ships as long as we're around. We'll drop the request, sir. You'll need everybody here for the defence of the airfield.'

'I've decided you can have your leave.'

'Sir?' they both cried.

'Er . . . sir,' Shilling added.

'But . . .' Chandler began.

'No buts, Mr Chandler. If you don't take that leave, you may not get the chance for some time. Jerry has kept us waiting for two weeks. He may do so for much longer. I'm even giving you an extra day. Take seventy-two hours . . .'

'What if he attacks while we're away?' Chandler suggested.

'I'll have to hope he doesn't, or I'll live to regret

it. Besides, you two have been flying more hours than anyone else. I'd rather you had a break and returned refreshed, than have you go aloft fatigued and prone to mistakes. No use to me then. And what do you intend to do with your leave?'

'I've simply got to get my kit, sir,' Chandler explained. 'Look at me. I'm hardly my normal sartorial self.'

Johnstone gave a fleeting smile. 'It has been noticed that you're walking round looking like something even the cat wouldn't touch. I believe the only reason the station commander has not commented upon it is because you're up so often, you're hardly here to have a finger pointed at you. And you, young Bob? What are you to do with your leave?'

'Well, sir . . . um . . . Shippy's invited me to spend the weekend with his family.'

'Has he indeed? Then enjoy yourself. Do you good.'

'Yes, sir.'

'And don't let the side down, will you? Treat Miss Chandler as a gentleman should, even if her brother's a reprobate.'

Shilling gave a sheepish smile. 'Yes, sir.'

Chandler grinned.

'You're in luck, gentlemen,' Johnstone went on. 'The Anson's returning tomorrow with the CO aboard . . .'

'Oh no!' they both cried before they could stop themselves.

'I did not hear that, gentlemen,' Johnstone said severely. He was not smiling.

'No, sir,' they chorused. 'You did not hear that.'

He stared at them levelly. 'There is a fine line, gentlemen, which you do not cross.'

'Sir.'

'Now. As I was saying ... the CO returns tomorrow. See that you're aboard that Anson before it leaves. I'll expect you back here at the end of the seventy-two hours. I don't care how you make it. Just be here on time. I will accept no excuses.'

'Yes, sir,' Chandler said.

'No, sir,' Shilling said.

'Thank you, gentlemen. Enjoy yourselves.'

They made it to the Anson the next day, and their paths did not cross du Toit's. Whether by design or simply the way things turned out, they were very happy to miss running into him. Neither had looked forward to the possible encounter.

As the Anson, which had stopped just long enough to disembark du Toit, took off again, the squadron commander strode into his office and summoned Johnstone. He'd hung up his cap and was removing his greatcoat, when Johnstone entered.

'Any excitement while I was away?' he asked as he sat down behind his desk.

'Quiet as a church mouse,' Johnstone replied. 'The Hun's still on his tea break.'

'Coffee break.'

'Beg your pardon . . . ?'

'Coffee. They drink coffee over there.'

'Er . . . yes. I know.'

'So your theory's coming apart.'

Johnstone stared at his commander. 'I don't think so,' he said quietly. 'I think he's planning something particularly nasty to send our way.'

Du Toit looked palely back at him. 'Despite my own misgivings, I was prepared to go along with you for a while. But the extra patrols are using up fuel, and tiring the pilots. I'm letting this run for just a few more days, then it's back to the standard routine.'

'That's what Jerry would like, sir,' Johnstone pleaded. 'I'm certain he's been keeping an eye on all the activity . . .'

'How? He's not had an aircraft in the area.'

'Submarines,' Johnstone replied. 'And E-boats. All they have to do is come out at night, and listen. When Jerry's decided we've become fed up with patrolling ostensibly enemy-free skies, that's when he'll strike. I am certain of it. They're just waiting for the right moment. It's what I'd do.'

Du Toit looked unconvinced. 'But you're not Jerry. A few more days,' he repeated. 'Now to the reason I've been down to Norfolk. We're going to play host to some SOE people, for a mission to Norway. They'll also be needing a fighter escort there and back, for an ultra-low-level Lysander flight.

'In a way your patrols will be of some use, after all. They'll serve as good cover, when the time comes. Jerry will simply think we've decided to do some more stooging around, and won't pay much attention.' Du Toit had the grace to say this without a smirk. 'I'll fill you in on the details later, after I've reported to the station commander.' He stood up and began to get his coat. 'Anything else I should know?'

'I've given Chandler and Shilling seventy-two hours' leave. Chandler's invited Shilling home. They went off in the Anson.' Johnstone was almost gleeful.

Du Toit paused in the act of shoving a hand into a sleeve of the greatcoat. '*What?* By what authority . . . ?'

'Mine. In your absence I was the squadron commander. I took a command decision. They've been flying almost twice as many hours as the other pilots, volunteering for extra patrols. As you've just said, we don't want tired pilots. I felt they could do with a spot of leave.'

Du Toit continued to put on his coat in silence. He buttoned it deliberately, as if not quite trusting himself to speak. He took his cap off the hook, and clamped it on his head.

'Chandler took Sergeant Shilling to his *home*?' Du Toit sounded scandalized, and stared into an emptiness as he spoke.

'Yes.'

'He's got a young sister, hasn't he?'

'Yes,' Johnstone repeated. 'She's eighteen, or thereabouts.'

The pale eyes turned on Johnstone. 'Fine,' he said at last. 'They're such great pals, they can fly the escort for the Lysander. I'll be with the station commander if you need me.'

He brushed past Johnstone and went out.

The Anson took Shilling and Chandler all the way to Aston Down. It had stopped *en route* to pick up two further passengers who had kept to themselves, and who were bound for the same place.

Shilling and Chandler thanked the crew and climbed out, moving away from the aircraft as the other passengers disembarked. As things worked out, the Anson crew said they'd be back in three days. If Shilling and Chandler were present in time, they'd take them as far as Tain, in Ross-shire, from where they could make their own way back to their unit. It was far better than they'd hoped.

'This is perfect!' Chandler said against the noise of the engines. 'A stone's throw from where I live!'

'How far?'

'Perhaps a little more than a stone's throw, but we're practically there.'

Shilling looked about him. 'Better than a train journey any day. It feels almost like summer this far south. I was training here, not so long ago.'

'That makes two of us.'

'Wonder if my old instructor's still here . . .'

'No time to renew old acquaintances, old man. We've got just seventy-two hours and the clock began ticking when we took off. Let's see if we can cadge a lift.'

Chandler was good at cadging. They eventually found a supply lorry whose route passed within half a mile of the Chandler home. Six hours from the time they had taken off from Fort Town, they were walking up the drive to the house.

Shilling stared transfixed as they approached it. '*This* is your home?'

'Bit of an old shack, I know. But I do love the old thing.'

'A *shack*?'

Someone was running out of the house to meet them.

'Timmy! Timmy!' Susan Chandler cried with surprise and pleasure. She ran up to her brother and gave him a great hug. 'It's so good to see you! And I'm so glad you're all right. Mother knows you're here. I saw you arrive from her window.'

Then she stood back to look at Shilling, and at that moment he fell hopelessly in love.

'Susan,' Chandler said, 'meet Jack Shilling, terror of the Hun. Everybody calls him Bob, of course. Saved my life, old girl. Saw me embroiled in a pack of Messerschmitts, waded in and tore into them. If it hadn't been for him, I'd definitely not be here to see you today. Thought I'd repay the poor man by foisting my family upon him. I think we've got some room, haven't we?'

Susan held out a hand and smiled. 'I think we have. I'm not everybody,' she added to Shilling, 'so I'll call you Jack. Is that all right?'

Shilling took the hand, and thought it was the most wonderful hand he'd ever touched. 'Yes,' he said shyly.

'Oh good.' The hand lingered.

Chandler looked at them benevolently. 'There. Didn't I say you'd like her, Bob? I can see you're getting on,' he went on drily, 'so I'll go up to

Mother.' He glanced about him. 'No car. I assume Father's not been.'

She shook her head without looking at him.

Chandler glanced at their hands. 'You can let go, if you wish,' he suggested with some amusement and walked on.

'Oh!' she said, smiled self-consciously, and took her hand reluctanctly away. 'Let's . . . let's go in. So you saved Tim's life,' she continued as they walked.

'He makes it sound far more impressive than it was,' he said to her, thinking she had a beautiful voice that went right to his very soul.

'I'm sure he didn't. I think *you're* trying to make it sound less than it is. You must be very brave.'

'Oh, I don't know. Most of the time I think I'm scared, once I've got into combat.' He stopped talking suddenly. He'd never said that to anyone before; not even Chandler.

As if she understood, she turned to look at him. 'That's why I think you're very brave. And thank you for telling me.'

'I've . . . I've never said that to anyone before.'

'I know,' she said gently. She took his hand again, holding it fully. 'Come on. I'll show you a room I'm sure you'll like, then I'll give you a tour of the place.'

The room she'd chosen for him was so huge it

seemed to dwarf the four-poster bed, which was sumptuously covered. Though there was no fire going, the place felt warm.

'I'll get lost in that bed,' he remarked drily.

'It's very cosy under those bedclothes,' she said, smiling at him. 'I do hope you'll be warm enough. You could probably do with a good night's sleep in a proper bed. Those bunk things they give you can't be very comfortable.'

'You'd be surprised how comfortable they can be when you're tired.'

'I expect so.' She pointed to a door at the side of the room. 'A bathroom's through there. Spruce up if you'd like, then meet me down in the hall. Can you find your way back?'

'I'll find you,' he said. The words were out before he could do anything about it.

His boldness surprised him. It was as if some invisible hand had planted itself in the middle of his back and was pushing for all it was worth.

Her astonishing eyes seemed to widen slightly. 'I'm glad you were there when Tim needed help.'

'I'm glad I was there, and I'm glad he brought me here.'

She turned away, walked to the entrance to the bedroom and paused by the door to look back at him.

'I'm glad you came down to see us.' She shut the door quietly behind her.

Shilling found that his heart was beating wildly. She was not the first white girl he'd been attracted to. That dubious honour went to Ellen Bradley, sister of a schoolfriend in Jamaica when he was fourteen and a half and she exactly a year younger.

John Bradley was the son of the headmaster at the boys' school he'd attended; the same schoolmaster who'd helped him get into the RAF. The pubescent Ellen had seemed like a blonde angel to him. And when the Bradleys invited him to accompany them on beach picnics, he'd spend so much of the time admiring Ellen in her swimsuit that his friend would frequently be forced to drag him away to go swimming, or inshore spearfishing.

Then Ellen had grown up and married someone much older than herself, from a colonial banking family. It had been inevitable. She was always going to marry someone from the expatriate crowd; but it had broken his heart. He'd never let on. He'd even been invited to the wedding. As for John Bradley, he'd joined the Royal Navy, was commissioned and, the last Shilling had heard, was aboard the *Prince of Wales*.

Be sensible, Jack, he now thought. It will be Ellen all over again. She's bound to be already going out with some officer. You've got no chance, Sergeant.

And yet, and yet.

He went into the bathroom, which seemed almost as big as the bedroom, and freshened up. He returned to the bedroom and stood before a huge, full-length mirror, checking his best blue uniform. He patted at it, smoothed it down, stroked the wings he proudly wore.

On his feet were officer-pattern shoes he'd bought himself, anticipating a commission. But the commission had not come. So he'd thought he'd wear them only for special occasions. This was one such, and there was no one around to say he was improperly dressed. At the station, he always wore his flying boots.

'Anyway,' he said to himself in the mirror, 'sergeant pilots are only officers waiting to be commissioned. When? Ah. Now you've got me.'

He stroked the wings again. They were blooded wings now, as Hamish Johnstone would say.

He studied them, as if looking for answers to questions he did not even know. Bradley senior had put him on the path to those wings. He wondered how John was doing on his ship, and how Ellen was coping with married life.

'Not your problem any more, Jack boy,' he said to himself, and went out to find Susan.

She was waiting in the lofty hall. She seemed pleased to see him and looked at him appraisingly as he drew nearer.

'Quite the winged warrior,' she said. 'Do you like your room?'

'I still think I'll get lost in it, but yes, thank you. I like it.'

'Good. We aim to please.' She tucked her arm in his. 'First, I'll present you to Mother, then the guided tour.'

He held back. 'Your mother? Oh God.'

She tugged at him. 'Don't look so worried. She won't bite. She wants to thank you personally for looking after Timmy.'

'Where is he, by the way?'

'Don't sound so hopeful. He's having a bath. You're on your own. Well, not strictly alone. I'm here to give you moral support?' She smiled at him, and held firmly on to his arm.

It was obvious where Susan's beauty had come from. Helen Chandler bore her illness stoically and despite the etchings of pain, the beauty of her face was there for all to see.

She was lying back in bed, propped up by large pillows. Her head turned towards the door as they entered, her eyes showing no surprise when she saw the house guest. Shilling assumed that Chandler had warned her about what to expect.

But Shilling warmed to her when she patted the side of the bed. 'Sit here so I can see you properly.'

Susan released his arm as he went over to the bed, but she stayed close. Shilling sat down carefully, and Helen Chandler laid the hand on his arm.

'You're terribly young to do all those things Timothy has said,' she remarked.

'Some are younger than I am, Mrs Chandler.'

'I know,' she said quietly. 'Awful thing this war. It's taking all our young people. Thank you for letting us have Timothy back.'

'I just happened to be in the right place at the right time,' he said awkwardly. 'If the situation had been reversed, he'd have done the same for me.'

The pain-filled eyes looked deep into him. 'Oh dear. I've embarrassed you.'

He smiled sheepishly at her.

'What a nice little smile,' she said. 'Don't you think, Susan?'

'Mother! You're embarrassing him even more. I'd better drag him away.'

'All right. Desert me, if you must. You will come to see me before you leave, won't you, Jack?'

'Yes, Mrs Chandler.'

'And call me Helen. None of that "Mrs Chandler" nonsense. You're not a servant.'

'No, Mrs . . . er Helen . . .'

But the invalid was already closing her eyes. Susan again took his arm and led him out, closing the door quietly behind them.

'Sometimes,' she began to explain as they moved away, 'she gets so easily tired.'

'She's a lovely lady.'

'She likes you very much.'

'Oh?'

'This is the first time I've heard her tell any young man with me to call her Helen.'

There it was. Any young man. She was going out with someone, as he'd thought.

'Consider yourself very privileged,' she was saying.

'I do,' he said.

For all sorts of reasons.

She showed him all over the magnificent house. It took a long time, but he enjoyed being with her so much he would not have cared if it had taken for ever. From time to time he thought he could see her cast surreptitious glances in his direction, but assumed it was just his overheated imagination.

'And that's it,' her voice cut into his daydreams. 'Impressed?' She seemed to be teasing him.

'Very.'

'You really do mean that, don't you?' she said, looking at him with dilated pupils. 'You don't seem to be saying that just for effect.'

'It is a very beautiful house.'

'And the people in the house?'

I'm drowning in her eyes, he thought, slightly deliriously.

He was saved by a voice saying loudly, 'Ah, there you are! Enjoyed the tour, Bob?'

Chandler, in a smart uniform, was coming towards them.

'Very much,' Shilling replied. 'Susan's a perfect guide.'

Chandler looked at his sister. 'Yes,' he drawled. 'You're not allowed to monopolize him today, Susan. You'll be having him all to yourself tomorrow.'

'Where're you going?' Shilling asked.

'Let's see. First, there's a certain young lady who's pining for my company . . .'

'He means Olivia Malmsbury, one of my friends. He couldn't stand her when they were younger.'

'Ah . . . but you see, little girls do grow up.' Chandler grinned at them. 'And,' he continued, 'I've also got to find out where my kit's been sent to, if anywhere. It will be a busy day.'

'What will you do for transport?' Shilling asked. 'Is there another car?'

'No . . . but there's a motorcycle,' Chandler said brightly. 'A Brough.'

'That thing,' Susan said dismissively. 'Will it run?'

'It certainly will. Donald's fixed it while I've been away. Runs sweetly, sister mine.'

Late after dinner that evening, when it was time for bed, Shilling called Chandler into his room.

'You look agitated, Bob,' Chandler began, well mellowed by good wine from his father's excellent stock. 'Tell old Shippy what's on your mind.'

'Is there a sidecar on your motorcycle?'

Chandler frowned. 'Thinking of deserting the ship?' He weaved slightly.

'It isn't like that.'

'Then . . . then what precisely is it like? Woo! Hope Father doesn't miss that wine. Marvellous stuff. So. Bob. What ails you?'

'Shippy, I don't know how to say this . . . but . . . but . . . oh, this is really difficult. What I'm trying to say . . . Look. It's Susan. I can't seem to stop thinking about her.' The last words came out in a rush.

'I did notice your eyes took on a glazed expression every time you looked at her. If it's any consolation, old boy, she had a similar look upon the visage that apparently has you in such thrall. I . . . I think I was

a sort of gooseberry tonight, if you see what I mean.'
Then Chandler smiled crookedly. 'Are you telling
me, oh slayer of Huns, that a man who can spot a
109 when it is but the size of a gnat upon the vast sky
– oh, I am a poet tonight – completely failed to spot
my sibling's earnest glances *all* evening? For shame!
Anyway, no sidecar. 'Night.' Chandler wove his way
out of the room, chuckling.

9

It was breakfast for two, the smell of freshly made coffee making it an enticing start to the day.

Chandler had set off early, long before Shilling was awake. As he now approached the table, Shilling looked at once embarrassed and apologetic.

'Good morning,' Susan said, greeting him with a bright, warm smile. 'That's your chair opposite.'

'Good morning,' he echoed uncertainly as he took his seat, remembering sharply what Chandler told him about her during their late-night chat in his bedroom. He thought she looked even more wonderful than before. 'I'm sorry to be so late. I slept like a log. The bed was so . . .'

'No need to apologize, Jack. The whole idea of your being here is to enable you to relax for a few hours. I looked in on you once. You were so fast asleep, I didn't want to disturb you.'

'You didn't. I never heard you come in.'

She gave him another smile, quick and fleeting

but with plenty of warmth. 'I've made some coffee. It's the real article. Father got given rather a lot by an American . . . admiral, I think he was. I thought you might like some.'

'Yes, please.'

He looked at her hands as she poured. They were as glorious as ever, the fingers long and tapered, with just a hint of plumpness about them.

She noted his look and was pleased.

Most of the breakfast passed in a gentle, leisurely silence as they ate, each simply pleased to be in the other's company and enjoying it. From time to time, one would pass a slice of toast to the other, or hold a cup out for more coffee, or pass the home-made jam, and so on. Sometimes their hands touched. When that occurred, Shilling swore he felt an electrical charge go through him.

They tried desperately to avoid looking directly into each other's eyes; but at times they would turn and find their gazes locked upon each other. Once, she blushed swiftly from her neck to the roots of her hair, a brief colouring that excited him.

After nearly an hour of this, Shilling could contain himself no longer.

'Susan,' he began, sounding as if he'd just run a mile. 'I've . . . I've got to . . . I don't know what's come over me. I'm Shippy's friend, I'm a guest in your house, you're his sister, and . . . It's the war, you see. One day we're there, and the next . . . What I'm trying to say . . . Oh, I'm making a real mess of this. What I mean . . . When I saw you for the first time yesterday, something happened to me. I just felt I couldn't leave here without telling you. And you'll probably be so offended . . . I'll have breached the rules of hospitality . . . You're probably seeing an officer anyway . . . I don't think I could bear not to see you again . . . but we've got to get back to the squadron tomorrow, so today is all we've really got . . . And I've only just met you for the very first time in my life . . . Hours . . . that's all we've known each other . . . And . . . I *knew* it. I've made a mess of . . .'

Then he realized that the hands he already loved so much were holding his. He stared at them, not daring to believe it. He couldn't be so lucky.

'Jack,' she began softly. 'You didn't have to say all that. I already know. When you looked at me yesterday for the first time, I knew too. Perhaps it is because of the war. Perhaps it's because when I heard what Timmy said about how you came to his rescue, and I realized how we could have lost him so easily, I decided that if what I was feeling so suddenly had any meaning, *I* had to tell you; even if you never plucked up the courage to say anything to me. I think Timmy knew very early on, what was happening. I know he's gone to see

Olivia, but I believe he left earlier than was strictly necessary, to give us as much of the day as possible. Timmy's like that.'

She made a reflective little sound. 'We might never have met. Before Timmy joined your squadron, I was very keen to go out and do my bit. But with Father already involved in war work and Timmy off to the Air Force, that left me to stay with Mother. So I was here, waiting for you, when you came to see us.'

She was still holding on to his hands. He looked at her, not daring to speak.

'What I'd like to do,' she went on, 'is spend the whole day with you . . .' She took a deep breath. '. . . in your room.'

His mouth hung open. 'I . . .' he began at last. 'I . . . do you know what you're saying?' He said this in a whisper, as if the big table was fully occupied.

She still did not let go of him, nor did she turn her eyes; but she was blushing again.

'I know.' It was simply said.

We can't, he wanted to say. I can't betray Shippy's hospitality like this.

But no words came. Everything was focused on the warmth of the hands that were clasping his.

He tried to delay the inevitable. After breakfast, they went for a walk down the drive then along the road towards the village. They met villagers who all seemed to know Susan and who looked at him with neutral curiosity until his greatcoat – which he wore unbuttoned – swung open when he moved, to briefly reveal his wings. Then the smiles came out. Being a pilot was OK.

Every so often a variety of RAF aircraft from the nearby training units roared overhead at differing altitudes. He wondered how many of the eager trainee pilots would survive the war. Then he put the thought out of his mind.

They turned round before the edge of the village and headed back for the house, scrupulously avoiding holding hands until they were within the grounds once more. Back at the house, Susan went to check on her mother, while Shilling went up to his room.

He removed the greatcoat and hung it up, then removed his tunic and put that over the back of a chair. He then began to nervously pace the room. A short while later, a soft knock made him jump. He went to the door and opened it.

Susan stood there, eyes wide, but with a determined look on her face.

'Mother's asleep,' she said, entering and softly closing the door by leaning gently against it, and pushing it with her behind as he slowly backed further into the room. The wide eyes remained locked on his. 'I'll leave if you tell me you don't want me.'

He said nothing.

She went close and put her arms about him, then with a great sigh, allowed her body to relax against his. Hesitantly at first, almost fearful, he brought his own arms about her. They held each other for long minutes, saying nothing as they stood there in the middle of the bedroom. Then she raised her mouth to his and kissed him gently.

It was at first an uncertain kiss, hesitant, for she was a little frightened by the speed with which it was all happening.

Then the gentleness of the kiss began to grow in intensity as he responded to the slow movement of her lips against his. They drew away from each other, staring and breathing hard, standing like that for some moments, knowing they would soon be crossing the point of no return.

Then a strange, low and long drawn-out sound came from him. He might have actually said something, but whatever it was, no recognizable words came out. She gave a soft cry as he grabbed at her, drawing her so tightly to him that she felt as if all the breath had been squeezed out of her. Kissing and staggering, they stumbled towards the bed.

She hauled at his tie, loosening it and pulling it off, then unbuttoned his shirt so that it hung open. They paused once more, now against the bed itself. With great deliberation she reached beneath her skirt, raising it slightly, and pulled down her knickers. The brief flash of her pale thighs sent a jolt through him.

She watched him closely, sensing hesitation.

'Don't change your mind now,' she told him, colour burning in her cheeks.

'I won't,' he said hoarsely and reached for her, pulling her to him once more.

The vigour of this action caused them to fall across the four-poster, rolling so that she was now beneath him.

He was not sure how or when the lower part of his body became unclothed. All he could remember was that he was entering her and she gave a sudden sharp squeal as he met resistance; but she wouldn't let him stop and the squeal became a long, high-pitched sigh that sounded repeatedly.

He felt as if his entire body was being pulled into her, making him want to stay in there for ever. Long, long after, when they were still, he kissed her damp forehead, and her cheeks, and her lips, and her eyes until he felt himself growing within her once more.

They lay beneath the bedclothes, clasped tightly to each other.

'I love you,' he said. 'I don't know whether people can fall in love so quickly; but I know how I feel.'

She held on tightly to him. 'And I love you,' she told him softly.

Chandler did not return that night. Susan spent the night with Shilling, leaving his bed in the early hours of the morning.

Chandler reappeared in time for breakfast. He'd located his kit, he said, which he'd had taken on to the airfield to await the arrival of the Anson. He said nothing about where he himself had spent the night.

After breakfast, Donald arrived with the car but not with the man of the house, who had remained behind at one of the aircraft factories. Donald offered to drive them to the airfield, and Shilling went up to say goodbye to Helen Chandler.

'Don't get killed, will you, Jack?' she said to him.

'I'll do my very best not to.'

'And please look after Timothy.'

'Always.'

'Come. Kiss me.'

He leaned forward to kiss her gently on the corner of her mouth. As he left, he was certain she already knew all about what had happened with Susan, without having been told by anyone.

Saying goodbye to Susan was terrible for him.

They stood awkwardly by the car while Chandler looked discreetly away. Donald, already behind the wheel, looked straight ahead.

Then she threw inhibitions to the winds and hugged Shilling tightly, squeezing her body against his, as if wanting an imprint of him.

'Please don't forget me,' she whispered in his ear. 'Please!'

'Never!' he vowed. 'I can never forget you. I only know that I love you,' he whispered to her, and felt a warm wetness on her cheek.

'Oh, I love you, love you, love you!' she murmured. She trembled slightly against him, stirring memories of the night.

Then he quickly let her go and got into the back of the car.

Chandler gave his sister a tight hug, then got in next to Shilling. Both looked back as the car moved off.

She stood there, receding, looking vulnerable and alone.

It wasn't until they were at the airfield waiting for the Anson that Shilling brought up the subject of Susan. At first he was not sure how to handle it. Chandler had not seemed perturbed; but friend or not, you never knew. What had taken place had occurred, had been so quickly . . .

'I must get through this war,' he said.

Chandler looked at him steadily. 'For Susan?'

'For Susan.'

'I won't ask what happened.'

'I won't tell you.'

'Don't expect you to. She's a big girl now.' Chandler gripped his friend's shoulder briefly. 'Knew you'd like her; but I must say the two of you fair took the wind out of my sails with your speed.'

'Do you object?'

'Good Lord, Bob. Of course not!'

'That means a lot to me.'

'Now don't you go soft on me,' Chandler said gruffly.

They grinned at each other, still friends.

While Shilling and Chandler were in the air on their way back north, Susan entered her mother's room.

Helen Chandler was awake, but slightly drowsy. However, she was still able to look at her daughter with some lucidity.

'You've been crying,' she said. 'For Timothy? Jack? Or both?'

'For both of them.'

'But a little more for Jack?'

'Oh, Mother . . . have I gone mad?'

'I doubt it,' Helen Chandler said, face creasing slightly as she coped with a spasm of pain.

'But I only met him a few hours ago!'

'Perhaps the war has lent a certain . . . urgency to your feelings . . . but that isn't the real problem, my dear. Have you considered all aspects of . . . this? Jack is a wonderful, lovely young man and in a perfect world you would both be very happy. But this is not a perfect world . . . and . . . there are too many people around without the benefit of your generosity . . . of spirit . . .'

'Are you saying I should stop seeing him?'

'Of course not, dear child. And I'm certain I couldn't stop you if you wanted to continue; so I wouldn't even try. I simply want you to know what to expect. Are you strong enough? You'll need to be.'

'I am,' Susan said firmly.

'And what will you do about Giles Linscombe?'

Linscombe was a Royal Marine lieutenant who came to visit every leave, and who had carried a torch for Susan even before he'd entered the service.

'I'm not in love with him, Mother. I never have been, and he knows it. I've never led him on.'

'Then I'm in your corner, my dear.' Helen Chandler closed her eyes. 'And so is Timothy. And even your father . . . will be.'

Susan hugged her sick mother gently. 'Oh, Mother,' she said, voice barely above a whisper. 'I do hope Jack will be safe.'

But Helen Chandler was asleep.

They arrived at Fort Town in the dark, at six in the evening. Master cadger Chandler had managed to marshal the services of the Home Guard this time, and had got them a lift on a supply lorry that was heading in the general direction of the station. The driver was kind enough to make a detour to take them right to the station gates.

They thanked him profusely as they climbed down.

'Got to keep you boys up there!' the driver said cheerfully, then turned the lorry round to continue his journey. He was old enough to be their father.

They collected Chandler's kit and trudged past the barrier and on to the station. The sentries, guns at the ready, shone soft torches at them, stared, then saluted on seeing there was an officer present.

'Well, the buildings are still standing,' Shilling commented, peering at the shapes in the gloom of the blackout. 'Jerry has not yet paid his visit.'

'Glad we didn't miss anything,' Chandler said.

Whatever the bush telegraph that had hummed

its message, the squadron car turned up soon after, with Creddon inevitably at the wheel.

'I don't think he ever sleeps,' Chandler remarked gratefully as the car drew to a halt and Creddon got out.

Creddon saluted. 'Had a nice leave, gentlemen?'

'We did, thank you, Two-Wheel,' Chandler replied. 'Anything exciting happen?'

'No, sir,' Creddon answered. 'You two were not here.'

'You *missed* us,' Shilling said.

'Yes, Sarge. We did. Dull around here with you gentlemen gone.' He picked up the kit and stowed it in the boot.

'You say such nice things, Two-Wheel,' Chandler said as they got in. 'Welcoming us back to the old place.'

'The cold, old place,' Shilling corrected, tightening his greatcoat about him.

'Some things don't change, Sarge,' Creddon said, starting off with a crunch of gears.

'We're home,' they chorused.

They went straight to the squadron and found Johnstone in his office. He looked pleased to see them.

'Had a good leave?' he asked.

'Yes, thank you, sir,' they replied together.

'As you've no doubt observed, the Hun is still putting off his visit. We're doing patrols, but only the standard ones. The CO's aloft at the moment, with Hardacre.'

'No one else, sir?' Shilling asked, very much surprised considering what the deputy CO had said about the imminent raid, before their leave.

Johnstone shook his head.

'We'll be into our flying kit as soon as we've dumped our stuff,' Chandler said. 'Just in case. May we warm up our kites?'

Johnstone's eyes lit up. 'No reason why you can't check over your aircraft. After all, you have been away. But don't take off. Got all your kit, Mr Chandler?'

'Yes, sir,' Chandler replied. 'It had somehow got re-routed, but I rescued it in time.'

Johnstone smiled tightly. 'Glad to have you back, gentlemen, *and* within your time limit. Impressive.'

They grinned at him, saluted and went out.

There was no raid that night, but Shilling and Chandler stayed close to their warmed-up machines, keeping themselves warm by the stove in a nearby Dispersal hut.

At about 0400 hours, Johnstone sent them word to stand down and they went off to bed. Each fell asleep with only his Mae West removed.

Chandler met Shilling outside the sergeants' mess just after breakfast.

'Tired?' he asked.

Shilling shook his head. 'I'm fine.'

'Good. The CO wants to see us.'

'Suddenly I don't feel so fine.'

'Cheer up. He can only shoot us.'

'What have we done?'

'God knows.' Chandler looked about him. 'We seem to have beaten Two-Wheel today. Let's walk.'

Then they heard the sound of a car.

'You were saying?' Shilling said.

The car drew up. 'A lift to the squadron, gentlemen?' Creddon offered.

'We'd better give in,' Chandler said.

'Yes, thank you, Two-Wheel,' Shilling said, and they got in.

Du Toit looked at them balefully as they stood before him. He did not ask about their leave.

'At some time in the near future,' he began without preliminaries, 'you will be required to fly as escort for a very important mission. I will give you a full briefing closer to the time. Hold yourselves at readiness. There is no fixed date for this mission. Needless to say, all further leave for you two is cancelled until after the mission. This is not to interfere with your normal duties. Thank you, Mr Chandler. Sergeant.'

'Sir!' they said, saluted, and went out.

The CO's baleful stare remained on the closed door for long moments after they had gone. He still could not accept that Chandler had actually invited Shilling into his home. It felt like a betrayal.

They saw Creddon waiting expectantly outside the squadron hut.

'Thanks, Two-Wheel,' Shilling said. 'We're walking.'

'OK, Sarge.'

As they walked, they heard footsteps behind them. They paused and turned to look, and saw Johnstone hurrying to catch up. They saluted as he joined them. He waved his hand casually at his cap.

'I take it you've been told?' he began.

Shilling nodded.

'Yes, sir,' Chandler said.

'Any details?'

'No, sir.' It was Shilling this time. 'He said we'd be briefed later, nearer the date.'

'I see. I do know something of what the mission's all about,' Johnstone went on after a pause, 'but it's up to the CO to tell you. After he's done that, come and see me.'

They nodded thoughtfully, wondering what was so special about that particular mission.

Johnstone looked up at the sky. The day was reasonably bright, but there was good cloud cover for any hopeful raiders.

'It's a bandit sky up there,' Johnstone said to them. 'Are you both fuelled and armed?'

'As always,' Chandler replied.

Johnstone looked up at the sky once more. They half expected him to sniff at it like a gun dog.

'Warm up the aircraft,' he said briskly. 'I may want you aloft at short notice. In fact, I think I'll give the order to warm up *all* aircraft.'

They looked at him, sensing his agitation.

'You're making me very twitchy, sir,' Shilling said, giving the air above a fleeting scan.

'You ought to be. I am.'

At the Ju-88 unit, there was plenty of activity. The roar of engines filled the air. The forward escort Messerschmitt 110Es, with Zürst leading, were already airborne, as were the high-flying 109 escorts from the neighbouring fighter unit.

The Ju-88s, loaded with high explosive and with fuel for the long trip, were staggering into the air in a seemingly unending stream.

Stammheim would be leading the main 110 escorts, which would be taking off last. He stood by his aircraft, watching as the 88s lumbered off. Pfaffenhof was with him.

'Are you happy with Zürst leading the Es?' the commander asked.

Stammheim nodded. 'He's progressed beyond expectations. He is good. I don't know what happened at that unit he came from, and I don't want to know. But from my experience as a combat pilot and instructor, the man's a natural. That unit's loss was our gain. He's an excellent *Zerstörer* pilot.'

Pfaffenhof's eyes became hooded. 'Let's hope you're right and he destroys the enemy.'

'I am right. That's why I've put him up front.' Stammheim looked seriously at his commander. 'You're staking plenty on this raid, Friedo.'

'Yes. I am. But this is the right day for it. All the reports indicate that the Tommies have cut down their patrols. Their guard is down . . .' He glanced up at the sky. '. . . and we've got the perfect weather for it. *Hals und Beinbruch!*' He held out a hand.

Stammheim shook it. 'We'll hurt them today.'

'See that you do.'

Shilling and Chandler were still some distance from their aircraft when they heard a racing motor. Johnstone was still with them. All paused to look in the direction from which the sound was coming. The squadron car was bucketing towards them, Creddon seemingly intent on breaking every speed limit on the station.

They looked at each other, immediately alert. Creddon would neither be mad nor stupid enough to drive so quickly without very good reason. The car came to a skidding halt and Creddon leapt out.

'Sir!' he began to Johnstone. 'Message from Flying Officer Michaels. A Navy sub's reported seeing large formations of enemy aircraft joining with other formations and heading westwards.'

Johnstone glanced quickly at Shilling and Chandler. '*This is it!* Any precise direction?' he went on sharply to Creddon. 'Are they going for the ships? Or are they headed inland?'

'Still too far out to tell, Mr Michaels said, sir. He's told the Navy to give a running report.'

'Thank God for the Navy. The early warning has given us some extra time. Right, you two,' Johnstone said to Shilling and Chandler, who were already poised to go. 'Get airborne! Shilling has the lead. Any objections, Mr Chandler?'

'None from me, sir. Bob has the lead.'

'No. Wait.' Johnstone then spoke rapidly. 'I want the ninety-gallon drop tanks fitted to each of your aircraft. This will give you a grand total of 274 gallons. Plenty of endurance. You'll use the fuel in them to find the enemy formation, then remember to jettison them before engaging in combat, or you'll think you're flying a London bus, and the enemy will scarcely believe his luck. Reaching the enemy formation with plenty of fuel in reserve, even with a clean aircraft, means you can fight longer than he can, if he wants to complete his mission.

'*Find* that formation long before it gets over land. I'll have the entire complement of twenty-eight Hurricanes airborne. With you two, that gives us thirty. We'll make our numbers count. As we know more from the Navy, we'll update the bandit position and let you know, using the grid code. Check the position on your maps but do *not* acknowledge. Simply make your way there. The enemy will be listening and must not know the destination of the messages. Radio silence until battle is joined. Got that?'

'Yes, sir,' they both said.

'Harry the bastards, but stay out of trouble, if you can. Your job is not to fight them seriously before we've arrived, but to make them waste time and fuel chasing after you. Laden to the gills with fuel, the escorts won't be able to catch you. They wouldn't, or shouldn't under normal circumstances. So make life extremely difficult for them. Tie them up and disrupt their mission. We'll be following hard behind. You won't be alone for long.' Johnstone looked at them calmly. 'I'm not going to shake hands. I fully expect both of you to be still alive by the time we get to you.'

'Sir.'

'All right, gentlemen. You may now scramble!'

As they ran towards their aircraft, Johnstone turned to Creddon.

'Was the squadron leader still in his office?' he said as he climbed into the car.

'Yes, sir,' Creddon said.

'Very well, Two-Wheel,' Johnstone said as Creddon settled behind the wheel. 'Today, you'll get a chance to show us what you can really do with that car. First, get me back to my office, then find every pilot, wherever he is, and tell him to get to his aircraft, on my authority . . .' Johnstone paused as the car lurched off.

'The Tannoy will be going, but there's bound to be someone who won't hear. I want *every* pilot at his aircraft.'

'Yes, sir!'

The car squealed round a curve in the road. It felt as if it had done so on two wheels.

Once in his office, Johnstone immediately called Dispersal to order the fitment of the drop tanks to Shilling's and Chandler's aircraft.

'Be very quick about it, Flight,' he urged the flight sergeant in charge of the ground crew.

He then went into Michaels' office to see if there was further news from the Navy. There was plenty, and it was coming in steadily.

The Navy, primed by Michaels and taking no chances, had placed a sub on station, close to the enemy coast, from the very first warning. Despite the threat to the airfield, the Navy's first priority was to its ships and so the submarine had really been on watch for that purpose. The position had been continuously manned and rotated, with the duty sub remaining silent on the bottom, listening, for most of the watch period.

This was done by the very simple method of floating a tethered passive detector to the surface to listen for aircraft, and a constant listening watch kept on the hydrophones, for the approaching sounds of any surface vessels; at which point the detector would be hauled down to the sub. It was one such submarine that had detected the airborne sounds of Pfaffenhof's armada.

'I'm going in to the CO,' Johnstone now said quickly to Michaels. 'Come with me, and bring that stuff with you.'

Johnstone knocked on the door and they entered to du Toit's response.

Puzzled, the CO looked up at them. 'Yes, gentlemen?'

Michaels gave Johnstone his notes, then moved a little to one side.

Johnstone passed the notes to du Toit. 'It's happening, Paul. The raid has taken off.'

Du Toit studied what Michaels had written. 'When did this come in?'

'It's still coming in.'

Just then, the double bark of two Merlins starting up came clearly to them.

Du Toit looked up from the sheets of paper. 'Who's about to take off? I gave no . . .'

'Shilling and Chandler . . .'

'*What?* By whose authority? Do I have to keep reminding you who's in command here?'

This time Johnstone decided to let his exasperation get the better of him. '*Dammit, Paul!* We're about to be raided! But there's still time to prepare and get our aircraft up. I'm trying to *save* the squadron and if you don't get a move on, you'll have no command left! I need your permission to get all the Hurricanes airborne. I'm going up myself.

'Shilling and Chandler are off to engage in a delaying action, to force the fighter escorts to waste their fuel and buy us some time. I can only hope they last until we get there. I've already sent Creddon to warn all the pilots, but we need to get the Tannoy going, and to warn the station commander. I'll tell you something else: if we don't save this place, that Norwegian mission is off. There'll be no station, and no fighters for the escort.'

Johnstone stopped, waiting for du Toit's reaction. He saw the South African's lips tighten and knew that he hated admitting that Johnstone had been right all along. Du Toit was trapped. Do nothing, and he would be held responsible for the destruction of the station and its aircraft. But going Johnstone's way meant having to accept that he'd failed to read the situation properly.

Having a very good idea of what was going on in the other men's mind, Johnstone decided to go for peace overtures.

'Look, sir,' he began, 'I'm your deputy. It's my job, my *duty*, to watch your back. I'd be failing in that duty if I did not do everything possible within my power to ensure the safety and the continuing integrity of the squadron as a fighting force. I am not trying to undermine you.'

There was a slight pause before du Toit spoke. Michaels watched almost clinically, as the squadron commander came to terms with what he had to do.

'You seem to have everything in hand, Hamish,' du Toit said at last. 'Carry on. I'll brief the station commander.'

'Thank you, sir. Will you be flying with us?'

'Just you try and stop me.' There was the barest hint of a smile in the pale eyes.

'I wouldn't dare,' Johnstone said.

10

Shilling and Chandler took off just as the Tannoy began to blare its warning, summoning all pilots to their aircraft.

They eased the Hurricanes off the runway and went into a steady, shallow climb, mindful of the extra weight of the drop tank beneath each wing. They held power at a steady 140mph. The aircraft could not be dived, nor spun – even inadvertently – while those tanks were still attached. Any sign of enemy aircraft, even before they got to where the bombers were, would necessitate instantly dumping the tanks.

Having taken off on the main tanks, they switched to the first drop tank and turned off the main tanks. They rose above the cloud cover and settled into a steady speed, in level flight, of 170mph – the best recommended speed for maximum range. The intention was to use the fuel from the drop tanks to get as far as possible, before jettisoning became necessary.

Shilling found he'd had to retrim the aircraft only slightly to relieve the load on the stick. As long as he did nothing spectacular, the Hurricane would happily cruise along until it ran out of fuel.

He looked across to his right and slightly over his shoulder to where Chandler was keeping perfect, close formation. Chandler gave him a little salute.

He responded with a thumbs up. Then a voice came through on the headphones.

'Baker to Papa Seven! Repeat. To Papa Seven!'

He signalled to Chandler by touching the right headphone. Chandler nodded, acknowledging receipt of the message. Shilling checked grid square Papa Seven on his map and went into a gentle turn to the left to settle on to a heading that took them slightly north-east.

He glanced at the square panel set centrally in the full instrument panel itself. Positioned vertically beneath artificial horizon, was the direction indicator: the compass. Within a slot in its top half, the course markings rotated until the marking for 65° settled beneath the course indicator line at its centre.

Zürst was flying the lead two-aircraft element of his six 110Es, well ahead of the main Ju-88 force. His aircraft, like all the Es, was equipped with eavesdropping equipment which the specially trained gunners operated. He'd heard the English message.

'Baker to Papa Seven.' What did that mean?

Feldwebel Johann Stolberg was the gunner-operator and Zürst decided to check with him.

'What do you make of that, Johann?'

'Could be anything. It's a ground station calling.'

'But why doesn't Papa Seven reply?'

'Radio silence?' Stolberg suggested.

'Baker, whoever he is, would know that. So why break it?'

'An emergency, perhaps.'

'Keep listening,' Zürst ordered. 'We might hear Baker again.'

'*Zu befehl, Herr Leutnant.*'

As he led his escort flight towards the enemy target, Zürst felt an unease about the strange radio call. Why hadn't the Tommy responded to his comrade? Or was Papa Seven unable to because he'd already been shot down? Was there a battle going on somewhere else, and they'd simply eavesdropped on one of the transmissions?

He checked his immediate surroundings. His 110s were nicely spread out in pairs. Below them and some distance behind, the heavily bombed-up 88s would be blackening the cloud bank with their numbers. Above the 110s, the 109s would be weaving, watching out for the first signs of enemy fighters.

Zürst felt itchy.

'Keep a good lookout, Johann,' he told the gunner.

'I'm the eyes in the back of your head,' Stolberg said.

Zürst smiled to himself.

Stolberg was the sort of person he liked having around. A no-nonsense man from Hesse, he was a few years older and had never bought the Nazi fanaticism. Being in the Luftwaffe was more like a job to him. The enemy had to be fought, and that was it. As for the rest of the Party propaganda, he was not interested. He'd once confided to Zürst that if he ever came across a wounded or unarmed Tommy, he would do his best to ensure the enemy serviceman never fell into the hands of the Gestapo or SS, and would even try to let him escape if that was the only way to prevent that happening.

Zürst had warned him to keep such dangerous thoughts to himself, but had silently found himself in sympathy with the view.

'Baker to George Nine! Repeat. Baker to George Nine!'

'There it is again, Johann. What now?'

'It sounds as if this Baker has lost his little sheep,' Stolberg said with a chuckle.

'That was Bo-peep.'

'I still think we're listening to calls to lost sheep.'

There was no reply from George Nine.

'The more they lose,' Stolberg went on, 'the better for us.'

'There's something I don't like about this,' Zürst remarked.

'Your hair's itching?'

'Yes. I never ignore that. Something's not quite right.'

As Shilling had led Chandler into another change of course, heading for grid square George Nine, he'd wondered what an enemy eavesdropper would make of those terse messages.

He checked his fuel. Plenty to spare.

They were still on the drop tanks, so the main and reserve tanks were full. At 20,000 feet, where they now cruised at zero boost and on weak mixture, and holding the rpm at between 2000 and 2300, consumption was some thirty-eight gallons per hour. During combat, with the mixture rich and full boost at 3000 rpm – though not continuous for too long – the consumption could rocket to a staggering 115 gallons per hour.

The fuel pressure light for the drop tank in use came on. Time to change to the second tank. At the same moment he turned on the reserve tank. This would prime the system and help the engine pick up more quickly when fuel intake was changed to the second underwing tank. The engine sang lustily. He now turned off the reserve and switched to the unused drop tank. The change-over went smoothly. He knew Chandler would have gone through the same procedures.

Their course was now 085, almost due east. There was still nothing in sight. They were well over water now, and approaching enemy skies. There should be a sighting soon.

Shilling scanned the air about him continuously.

'Baker to Baker Six! Repeat. Baker to Baker Six!'

The new grid square was now almost due north. Shilling banked into a wide, gentle turn, closely followed by Chandler's aircraft. He had a feeling that they'd be getting that sighting soon.

Nearly time to dump the tanks.

'Baker seems to have lost someone from his own formation,' Stolberg commented. 'Where can this battle be taking place?'

Zürst studied the sky about him. The high-flying escorts had given no warning, so wherever the battle was, it was not close enough to worry about. Were they listening to an enemy bombing raid in progress?

He checked his watch. There was still a long way to go to the target. All the aircraft were heavy with fuel. Making contact with the enemy so soon would not be a good thing.

'Baker, any time!'

Shilling knew what that meant. They were about to make contact with the vanguard of the enemy formation.

He turned on the main tanks, then switched off the right drop tank. Most of its fuel had gone by now, so he wouldn't be discarding much of the valuable fluid. It was time to dump.

He turned to look at Chandler's aircraft. His friend's helmeted head was turned towards him. He made a chopping motion with his right hand. Chandler nodded, acknowledging it was time to jettison.

Shilling reached to his right, just aft of the windscreen de-icing pump, where both the drop tanks' fuel cock and the jettisoning lever were mounted together, and checked that the fuel cock was off. They wouldn't jettison otherwise, and with good reason. No one wanted an aircraft awash with spilled fuel.

The cock was off. He reached further sideways

for the lever and pulled it down. The tanks went smoothly.

He glanced across at Chandler. The tanks were still attached to the aircraft. Chandler seemed to be working furiously. The tanks had jammed. That was very bad news indeed.

Chandler looked at him. Shilling raised a hand in query. Chandler shook his head, and made a cutting motion. He couldn't get the tanks to release.

Shilling wondered whether Chandler had checked the fuel cock.

For valuable seconds they flew steadily while Chandler continued to work at jettisoning the offending tanks. Then suddenly they were tumbling away. Chandler gave him the thumbs up. Shilling heaved a sigh of relief. He could find out what happened later. There was more serious business at hand.

'Baker, *any time*?' Zürst repeated.

'Perhaps they mean answer in your own time,' Stolberg suggested. 'They're getting desperate.'

'I think not. It means something else. I *know* it. The question is . . . what?'

Zürst checked the sky about him yet again, but could see nothing to confirm the sense of urgency he now felt.

*　　*　　*

The crews of two Ju-88s at the head of the main formation got the shock of their lives when the rear gunner of one 88 spotted two shapes descending on them.

'*Spitfeuer!*' he yelled, and fired.

As if mentally linked to him, the guns on the other aircraft within his immediate vicinity opened up.

But the shapes continued to plummet down. It wasn't until just before one smashed into the canopy, killing him instantly, that he realized it wasn't a Spitfire.

The second drop tank from Shilling's Hurricane slammed into the next aircraft, causing the two 88s to veer savagely into each other. The resultant collision flamed into a vast, bomb-generated explosion that set off two more, consuming the four aircraft within seconds. Fiery pieces tumbled seawards.

By now the rest of the formation was darting about wildly, desperate to avoid the same fate. The airwaves were suddenly crowded with orders and counter-orders, directions and counter-directions, as the aircraft went into gyrating evasive manoeuvres, to dodge both the non-existent enemy fighters and each other. Two more 88s slammed together and went down. There were no chutes to be seen.

Suddenly Pfaffenhof's big strike was six bombers short.

Chandler's own tanks, because they had taken

so long to release, missed the entire formation completely. No one even spotted them.

'What the devil's going on back there?' Zürst demanded as frantic calls invaded his headphones.

'It sounds like an attack,' Stolberg replied.

Zürst again looked about him. The sky was empty of enemy aircraft. 'What attack? The 109s have said nothing . . .'

Then Stolberg saw something that made him come to the wrong conclusion.

'There *is* an attack!' he called, astonished that the enemy had found them so soon, and still so far from the target. '*Fighters! Coming down!*'

Shilling at last broke radio silence as he spotted the six aircraft.

'Me-110s,' he called to Chandler. 'They can't outmanoeuvre us, and they'll be heavy with all that fuel. Burn nicely too. Go through them. No turning fight as yet.'

Those who had seen the green boy pilot arrive on the station would have been astonished by the transformation. The boy had become the grown warrior.

'Roger,' Chandler acknowledged.

As the two Hurricanes plunged towards the last pair in the formation, Shilling noted that the lead pair were already turning to give battle. But they would be too late. The pass would have gone through by the time they'd got close enough.

He saw twinkling things tumbling. Drop tanks. Good. They were already cutting their range.

The leader had obviously given the alarm, for the rear pair were now beginning the break. But they were moving so slowly that Shilling had no difficulty in following through. He noted with satisfaction that Chandler had latched on to the other.

They flashed past the 110s, preceded by brief spurts of cannon fire. As they pulled up into a loop and looked down through their canopies, they saw that they had scored. The two 110s were falling steeply, both trailing black smoke.

'We don't follow to check the kill,' Shilling said. 'They're out of the fight. Let's go for the others.'

'I'm with you.'

Zürst saw what had happened, and felt sick.

He knew now what those baffling messages had been about. They had not been desperate roll calls, but *coded directions to the bomber force. The fighters had been directed like hunting dogs to their targets.*

That was the only sensible explanation. That was why the fighters had got to them well before they were approaching the target airfield. The enemy had *known, and had prepared an ambush*.

Zürst realized only too well the fix he was in. He hadn't dropped his own tanks, but the rest of his formation had. They would not make it to the target and back with the fuel left aboard, especially after engaging in combat so far from the objective. But by keeping his own fuel, he was sacrificing his own limited manoeuvrability even more.

The enemy fighters were employing hit-and-run tactics, and clearly had no intention of getting near his guns. Were their companions even now wreaking havoc among the bombers? And what were the 109s doing? Were they asleep up there?

The 109s were not asleep. On erroneously being informed that the formation was under attack, they had maintained altitude, searching for the rest of the attack force. They assumed that the 110s were already among those at lower altitudes.

Their baffled pilots looked about them, wondering where the rest of the enemy fighters had got to.

Both Chandler and Shilling were well aware of the devastating blow that could come from the 110, and as Zürst had correctly surmised, had no intention of allowing themselves to get within range of that lethal fall of shot if they could possibly help it. If the circumstances of combat dragged them there, then they intended to make their stay as fleeting as possible.

With that thought concentrating their minds, they went into a second attack, knowing that their first objective had been attained. The bomber force was in a state of confusion and the 110s were being forced to waste time fighting when they were not ready to do so.

The big question was: how long would it take them to realize they were being engaged by only two fighters and not a huge attacking force?

Shilling hoped it would take long enough to allow the rest of the squadron to arrive on the scene. If the enemy suspected the situation, all they'd have to do was dispatch a few fighters to tie up the Hurricanes, while the bombers forged on towards the target.

'So if we can deplete this lot further,' Shilling muttered to himself, 'every little will help.'

The enemy, he hoped, would not want to believe that two Hurricanes, so heavily outnumbered, would be insane enough to attack in the first place.

Let them think we are legion, he thought drily.

'They're coming back!' Stolberg called.

Zürst tipped the Me-110 on to a wing and

hauled it into a tight turn. Even laden as it was, he still got more agility out of it than the rest of his formation.

'Can you see any of their friends?'

'Just these two,' Stolberg replied. 'They're not coming for us. They're going after Hacher and Forsch. My God! They've got them! Hacher's aircraft is burning. I can't see what's happened to Forsch. They've cut us down, sir.' Stolberg's voice was full of shock. 'So quickly. There's just us and Bauer's aircraft left.'

Zürst was feeling both angry and helpless. It was clear they were not dealing with novice fighter pilots, but with a couple of aces who knew how to pick their opportunities and stay out of trouble at the same time. Well, they weren't going to get him. With great reluctance, knowing he would not now make it to the target, he dropped his tanks and turned to give battle.

But something was worrying at him, like a dog that would not let go.

'Call the bomber formation,' he instructed Stolberg. 'Ask them if they can see the enemy fighters carrying out the attack.'

Stolberg began to call the bomber leader.

He was gone, as well as his deputy. Stolberg got the third in command. They were now surrounded by Stammheim's 110s. For the moment there were no British fighters to be seen. The attack appeared to be over. The formation was continuing, if behind schedule.

'Call the top cover, Johann,' Zürst further instructed. 'Ask them about the enemy fighters.'

Stolberg did so.

'No enemy fighters up there, *Herr Leutnant*,' came the gunner's astonished report. 'What's going on?'

'What is going on, my dear Johann,' Zürst said grimly, 'is a gigantic bluff. Those two fighters are the *only* two.' But then, having been right so far, he made a serious miscalculation. 'They must have come upon us unexpectedly, and took the opportunity that presented itself. I thought a fighter force was being directed towards us. I was clearly mistaken. Tell the 109s about these two. Let them herd them towards us. We'll give those Tommies a taste of their own medicine.'

'Immediately!' Stolberg acknowledged.

Zürst now wondered how Stolberg would react if he came upon the Tommies who had just shot down four of the precious 110Es. Would he still try to save them from the Gestapo?

Shilling watched the three specks coming down from on high.

'Uh-oh,' he said to himself. 'Our game's up.' To Chandler, he said, 'Trouble.'

'I see them.'

'This is Baker,' Shilling broadcast, deliberately doing so openly. Johnstone would understand why. 'If ever we needed you.'

'On our way,' came Johnstone's voice crisply.

Zürst now found he had to rapidly adjust his earlier understanding of the situation.

'If ever we needed you.'

One of the fighters was Baker, but it was not the same voice that had earlier sent the messages. There *was* an attack, after all. He had been right about the ambush.

'Send to all formations!' he ordered Stolberg. 'There *is* an attack. The first one was a feint. The real one is on its way! Do this at once!'

'Yes, *Herr Leutnant*!' said Stolberg, and immediately began speaking to the bombers and the fighters.

The whole thing was coming apart, Zürst realized philosophically. How many British fighters were now committed to this main attack? Just by being in the vicinity, they had achieved their first goal. They were delaying the bombers and forcing the fighters to waste valuable fuel. Pfaffenhof's raid would not now make it and the primary concern was going to be survival.

He wheeled the 110 tightly round, and headed back for the bombers. Bauer followed close on his heels.

'They're breaking off!' Chandler announced.

It was true, the high-altitude fighters had turned away, and so had the remaining 110s.

'Was it something we said?' Chandler continued.

Something I said, Shilling thought gleefully.

'Must be,' he replied to Chandler. 'Or your armpits are at it again.'

He had no idea how far the squadron was from the bombers or how long it would take them to get there, but the enemy didn't know either and had turned back to await the onslaught.

'Let's follow the game,' he said, 'but hang back.'

'I'm with you,' Chandler said.

The squadron was in fact much closer than expected. It had been assembled in four flights of six aircraft in two formations of twelve, plus a further four, waiting to join up with Shilling and Chandler.

Du Toit was leading the first twelve. Before take-off he'd agreed with Johnstone that his formation would hit the bombers and any escorts with them, while Johnstone would take his own high, to deal with any others lurking at the upper altitudes. The other four, when eventually joined with Shilling and Chandler, would be freewheeling, attacking the subsequently scattered target aircraft wherever they found them.

They spotted the bomber formation and its medium-level escorts not long after Shilling's call.

'Red and Blue flights, tally ho!' du Toit called, and plunged towards the heavily laden aircraft.

Twelve Hurricanes flung themselves at the enemy formation like avenging angels. The quadruple cannon spat out deadly rhythms as they hurtled through, forcing some of the Ju-88 pilots to heave their aircraft into violent collision-avoidance action. This instinctive manoeuvre caused ripples throughout the enemy formation, making life even more hazardous as each aircraft tried desperately not to plough into the one next to it. This also ruined any chances of co-ordinating defensive fire.

Twelve Hurricanes came through unscathed on that first pass, but they left four aircraft blazing – one a 110 escort – and several trailing smoke. They wheeled for another go, splitting into sections of two and attacking from several directions at once.

*　　*　　*

Johnstone's formation had by then reached altitude and was snarling up the 109s. The combat described graceful contrail streaks across the cold sky. Every so often something twinkled downwards, trailing a tail of fire or smoke. At times the descent would come to an abrupt end as the object exploded in a distant and silent puff of vivid hues.

Zürst and Bauer had reached the bomber formation and immediately took on the Hurricanes.

Zürst found himself in pursuit of one and, using gravity to give the heavier weight of his aircraft more velocity in the dive, he was slowly drawing closer towards the British aircraft, whose pilot seemed unaware of his impending danger.

In the back of the 110, Stolberg was pinned against his harness as Zürst continued his headlong plunge. Stolberg grimly wondered whether his pilot had forgotten this was not a 109.

The Hurricane drew ever closer.

Zürst fired.

The effect was spectacular. The Hurricane, an aircraft that could take considerable punishment, simply came apart as a barrage of heavy shells ripped into it. Remnants floated away as Zürst now began hauling the big twin-engined aircraft out of the dive.

But another Hurricane had spotted them and was on its way down.

Still forced against his harness by the pressures of gravity, Stolberg could only watch helplessly as the Hurricane drew inexorably closer.

'Hurri . . . *Hurricane*!' he croaked against the pressure.

Zürst forced his head round to glance over his left shoulder, saw the enemy aircraft bearing down, and immediately relaxed the pull-out, slamming Stolberg against his seat as the centrifugal forces abruptly changed, rolled the 110 to the right, continued through and pulled again into an impossibly tight turn for such a big aircraft. The powerful Daimler engines howled in protest, but did not miss a beat.

Stolberg thought either he or the aircraft would come apart at the seams. Both were still in one piece, and the Hurricane had disappeared.

'You OK back there?' Stolberg heard.

'I've still got all of me,' he answered, 'but I'm not sure if everything's still in the right place.' He chuckled with relief.

'Well, it's back we go,' Zürst said.

Tell me something I don't know, Stolberg thought.

The four Hurricanes detailed to join up with Shilling and Chandler were flown by Chivers, Hardacre, Ellerton and Hank the Yank who wasn't.

Shilling saw them approach in a beautiful line astern to curve into position.

I'm in the lead of six aircraft, he thought, feeling slightly intimidated by this sudden responsibility.

It could not have been du Toit's idea, assuming du Toit knew at all. Shilling saw the hand of Johnstone writ large.

'Three pairs, gentlemen,' he said to them. 'Keep the leads you came with.'

He watched with satisfaction as they paired off smoothly.

'Attack in pairs and each man watch his leader's tail. But we work as a pack. Let's go!'

The combat lasted for fifteen ferocious minutes, at all altitudes.

When it was all over, half the bomber force was destroyed, and several more so badly damaged that they would not make it back. Those few that were completely unscathed, dumped their bombs over water and headed home at ultra-low level.

The escorts took a pasting too. Bauer went down, as did four of Stammheim's 110s. Many others were damaged.

Unexpectedly, the 109s took a real beating. They'd been pounced on when they'd been still encumbered by their extra fuel, by the more manoeuvrable Hurricanes of Johnstone's formation. The twelve four-cannon firestorms had thundered devastatingly.

Of the thirty Hurricanes, five would not be returning to Fort Town. Two had fallen to Zürst. Three others were seriously damaged but would stagger home, with two of the pilots badly wounded. Johnstone, du Toit, Chandler and Shilling survived unscathed.

Ellerton did not make it, having had the misfortune to pass only fleetingly, in pursuit of a 109, before Zürst's guns. The 109 escaped.

Hank the Yank was slightly wounded but his Hurricane was virtually untouched, save for the entry of the single shell that had gone out again, and whose passage had just creased his arm.

Shilling had now added – including the two 110s – two bombers and a 109 to his tally of kills. Chandler had his two earlier 110s and a bomber, plus at least two seriously damaged 109s, one of which would go down before making it to base.

Johnstone had polished off three 109s, while du Toit had downed three 88s. And so it went on.

The snow squadron had had a very successful day, and the raid had been turned back. It formatted on its leader and headed home.

11

There was both celebration and sadness at Fort Town. The squadron licked its wounds and settled down to the business of its standing patrols.

A week after the battle, Johnstone went into du Toit's office with a proposal.

He placed a sheet of paper on the CO's desk. 'Here are my recommendations for combat decorations and . . . I want to recommend Shilling for a commission. Will you back me?'

Du Toit looked at him. 'Are you mad? A *commission*? How do you think the men will take it?'

Johnstone stared at him disbelievingly. 'I can't accept you've just said that. Do we now make decisions based upon what we think the *men* might think?'

'I have the stability of the unit, its discipline, to consider. If the men react unfavourably to him as an officer, where will that leave us?'

'In fact the men hold him in very high regard.

They are mightily impressed by his scores, and even that epitome of narrow thinking, Nobby Clark, dotes on his aircraft. Has nothing that happened last week made any impression on you? Shilling performed outstandingly. First, he had to disrupt the raid with just Chandler to keep him company. Then he commanded a whole flight . . .'

'I agreed to let you give him that command . . .'

'Which he handled excellently . . .'

'. . . as a token of my appreciation for your . . . saving me from certain disaster . . .'

'My God, Paul! He *saved* the squadron. By hanging on out there until we were able to join in, he bought us valuable time. His score's far and away superior to many who've been in combat for a great deal longer than he has. He'll catch up with me soon. How can you continue to treat the boy like that? He *deserves* his commission.'

While Johnstone continued to fix him with an outraged stare, du Toit looked down at the paper.

'I see you've recommended him for the Distinguished Flying Medal . . .'

'If he'd been an officer I would have said the Distinguished Service Order or at the very least, the Distinguished Flying Cross. His score is greater than anyone else's who took part in that battle but because they're officers they'll be receiving crosses . . .'

'I'm recommending you for a bar to your DFC . . .'

'I don't want it, if you're going to continue treating Shilling like this . . .'

'I'd hoped we would have put an end to this conflict between us by now, Hamish. Especially after what you did for me.'

'I did it for the squadron too.'

'I accept that.'

'But you're not giving me much of a chance, are you? You've got this . . . this *thing* about our young sergeant.'

'What makes you think a recommendation from here will be acted on? It might languish in a pending tray somewhere. Has it occurred to you that our superiors may *not* want to make him an officer, and have absolutely no intention of ever doing so?'

'There's one way to find out.'

'They may not like to be put on the spot like that. They may not like *us* for doing so, good combat records or not.'

'I want you to consider it,' Johnstone insisted.

The pale eyes stared at him. 'I'll consider it,' du Toit said unenthusiastically. 'Anything else?'

'We'll need pilots to ferry the replacement Hurricanes. They can go down with the Anson that's bringing in the new pilots.'

'The ATS have been doing an excellent job of

ferrying. We wouldn't be thinking of two pilots in particular, would we? And would those same two pilots be allowed an overnight stay or two somewhere?'

Johnstone said nothing.

'Don't push me, Hamish,' du Toit went on. 'If, as I believe, you're thinking of Chandler and Shilling, the answer is no. I've already told them no passes, no leave, until after the Norwegian mission. If you must use squadron pilots for the ferry job, we've got many more.'

'After the two of us, they're our best. And even then I wouldn't place bets, especially where Shilling is concerned. I'd be sure they'd bring those aircraft up in one piece, whatever the weather conditions.'

'It's still no. But I will think about the commission,' du Toit added grudgingly.

Johnstone wasn't sure whether he believed that.

Across the water, the atmosphere at the Ju-88 unit was rather less celebratory.

Pfaffenhof was relieved of his command and sent eastwards. Stammheim was promoted to lieutenant colonel and given the command. Zürst received the Iron Cross First Class for his combat performance and his prompt action in warning the formation, thereby limiting the magnitude of the disaster. All the 110Es he lost were replaced. He was also given accelerated promotion and skipped a rank to go directly to captain. Stolberg was made a warrant officer.

Steinhausen, Zürst felt with satisfaction, would have his nose put out of joint by the news. But by then he may well not want to be associated with Pfaffenhof, who would now have the stench of failure.

Two weeks after receiving his new promotion and decoration, Zürst was called in by Stammheim.

'Despite our recent disaster,' the major told him, 'you're beginning to make the high-ups notice you. I've received orders to select you for a special defence mission. You and your *Zerstören* are being sent to Norway. You are still part of my unit, so consider this a detachment. Do good, and make *me* look good.'

Zürst grinned. 'You can depend on it.'

'And look after yourself up there. Don't let the Nazis get to you.'

'They won't.'

'Or the Norwegians, or Tommies.'

'*They* won't.'

It was evening at Fort Town.

Shilling lay on his bunk reading a letter from Susan. He would not be on patrol till the next day and he'd decided to reread all the letters she'd sent so far. He'd written to her a few times, but mindful of the censorship regulations, he had kept his letters vague. He did not want people reading about his true feelings for her. Besides, you never knew what interpretation they might give his words.

Susan had no such inhibitions. She poured out her feelings to him. He could only hope that anyone opening them before he did would have the grace not to read right through. He hoped it would be Michaels, the adjutant.

It was Michaels, and Michaels did display such grace.

There was a knock on Shilling's door.

'I'm here.'

Chandler poked his head through. 'Shilling, DFM, Sergeant, sir, are you reading those letters again?'

Shilling gave a self-conscious smile. 'I haven't got the gong yet. Anyway, you've got one as well.'

'*You* should be getting a DFC, at the very least. A little bird's told me someone's put you up for a commission.'

'I won't get it,' Shilling said philosophically.

'Steady on, old son. You don't know that.'

'*If* it's put through, which I doubt, it will be turned down.'

'Old Hamish won't let that happen.'

'Old Hamish, bless him, is just one man.'

'Well, to me, you're already an officer. What do they say about sergeant pilots?'

'Officers waiting for commissions,' they said together, and laughed.

'I'm also here with other news,' Chandler went on.

'Oh?'

'We're off patrols as of this evening. That show the CO told us about begins tomorrow.'

'We do the escort tomorrow?'

'No. It seems we see the CO and meet some people. That's all Hamish would say.'

'What do you think it could be about?'

'No idea, old son. But I'll bet you it's dangerous.'

The next day brought a surprise for Shilling.

A Lysander landed at Fort Town. When Shilling and Chandler were ushered into du Toit's office, where Johnstone and Michaels were also waiting, Shilling was astonished to see an old friend standing next to an unknown major.

'*Dan!*' he exclaimed happily, before bringing himself up short. 'Er . . . sorry, sir,' he said to du Toit.

Silverdale was grinning at him.

Du Toit studied them both, then asked, 'You two know each other?'

'Yes, sir,' Silverdale replied. 'We were at initial flying training school together. Bob went on to get his dream of flying fighters. I got the Lizzie.'

Shilling noticed the DFM and bar beneath Silverdale's wings. Flying the Lizzie was obviously not a cushy job.

'This makes things even better,' du Toit was saying. 'It will concentrate your mind to know you'll be responsible for your friend's safety, Sergeant. Flying Officer Chandler,' he went on, 'Sergeant Shilling, may I introduce . . . Major Marais, and of course, Flight Sergeant Silverdale. You will be escorting their Lysander to Norway – and back. Whatever opposition you may meet on the way, the Lysander is to make it back safely. That is your prime objective.

'You are to spend today with the major and the flight sergeant, who will give you all the information necessary to make your escort mission successful. You will discuss this with *no one* outside this office. Flying Officer Michaels has kindly agreed to make his office available for your discussions.

'The mission will be flown at night. Time on the ground for the Lysander at the destination point will be no more than two minutes; therefore get your clocks and watches perfectly synchronized. Should you be spotted by defending fighters, you are to ensure none get near the Lizzie. Diversionary missions will be flown by a number of units who have no idea of the true reasons for those operations. *Their* purpose is to keep the Hun fighters busy, as well as keeping his attention away from the real mission. But things can, and do, go wrong. That's where you come in. Your job is to tackle the problem if it arises. Let us hope it does not.'

With Marais and Silverdale, Shilling and Chandler went through every aspect of the mission that concerned them, several times over. Headings, changes of course, precise timings for such changes, altitudes at which each leg would be flown – all were gone over in fine detail until thoroughly absorbed.

Though neither Silverdale nor Marais gave them details of the real purpose of the Lysander's mission, they had no illusions about the dangers they would all be facing.

As the planning went on, Shilling began to realize the true nature of what was involved in flying the Lizzie into enemy territory. There were no public accolades for these Lysander pilots. They died unseen and unheard of. They ferried and rescued agents. They supplied resistance groups. They saved downed airmen; and they did so all alone, under the cover of darkness, with capture an ever-present likelihood.

He felt great respect for his friend Silverdale.

It was again evening by the time everything had been covered to the mutual satisfaction of all four participants.

Then Johnstone, who had put in an appearance towards the end, said, 'One final but vital point of great importance to you as escorts. The Germans have got some night-fighter versions of the Messerschmitt 110 which are deadly. While the standard day fighter can become easy prey for the Spitfire or the Hurricane, these things are truly dangerous at night. We have received intelligence – supplied by Major Marais – about the equipment some versions carry. They have both radio location and heat sensors and can track you without your knowing it.

'They also have a gun installation in the rear cockpit they call *Schräge Musik* – "slanting music". This nasty piece of work fires obliquely upwards, and is usually a twin 20mm cannon. Their trick is to sneak in from behind and beneath you, and let you have both barrels in the gut, so to speak, raking you from tail to nose as they go past. So every so often, check not only your tail but also your underbelly.

'Some versions have additional cannon in a belly pack. These are 30mm monsters, but they add weight. Their search antennae array also induces more drag, so in effect this is in your favour. The aircraft must handle like a pig. In the final analysis, however, it's your eyeball versus his sensors. He can home in on you with his radio location, or on the heat from your Merlin exhausts ... so watch it.'

Shilling and Chandler took the advice to heart.

'Well,' Shilling began when Johnstone had finished, 'after that little nightmare, I'm for a quick meal and then bed.'

The others agreed. Johnstone suggested they should eat in the squadron hut instead of the mess, and a plentiful supply of beef sandwiches and tea was brought, which they demolished.

Leaving Marais and Silverdale to finalize their own arrangements, Johnstone, Shilling and Chandler walked to the sergeants' mess.

'Feeling all right about this?' Johnstone asked Shilling.

'Yes, sir. Shouldn't be a problem. There and back.'

'Piece of cake,' Chandler added.

'Perhaps,' Johnstone said. 'But I meant what I said. Watch yourselves out there. Take no chances.'

Silverdale came in later. He'd been allocated the spare bunk in Shilling's room.

'Never thought we'd meet up again like this,' he said.

'And *I* never imagined the sort of hairy stuff you get up to.'

'It only seems hairy afterwards. The really brave people are those who've got to fight Jerry on the ground every day of their lives, in their own country. We can't begin to imagine what that's really like.'

A silence descended on them as they tried to visualize how it would be if the Battle of Britain had been lost and there had been an invasion. It did not bear thinking about.

Shilling found his thoughts on Susan and dared not imagine what could have happened to her.

'I've found me a girl, Dan,' he said.

'Good on you! She pretty?'

'Absolutely beautiful. Shippy Chandler's sister. Her name's Susan.'

'Oh ho! Nothing like keeping it in the family.'

'I'd like you to meet her.'

'I look forward to that. Sounds like you're truly smitten. I've got my own confession to make. I think I've found one too.'

'You *think*?'

'Let's say she has a rather hectic life at the moment. She has the most amazingly bright eyes I've ever seen. I hope you'll meet her one day too.'

'Sounds like *you're* smitten.'

They laughed.

''Night, old mate,' Silverdale said.

''Night.'

The two Hurricanes flew towards Norway in the darkness. They were carrying the ninety-gallon drop tanks to extend their range. The tanks would not be jettisoned until they were empty, unless they were forced to do so before engaging in combat.

The Lysander had long ago taken off, flying extremely low over the dark water. Neither pilot knew that in its rear cockpit Marais was now attired in the uniform of a lieutenant colonel of the Wehrmacht, and that he spoke fluent German.

Shilling found his admiration of Silverdale's prowess increasing. During the day he'd seen the swastikas on the cockpit of the Lysander, and had wheedled out of his old friend the circumstances under which they'd been gained. Silverdale had told him, though leaving all specific details of the Resistance fighters – including Bright Eyes – out of the tale.

Before take-off, Shilling had handed Johnstone a letter to be sent to Susan, if anything happened to him.

'I know I shan't have to send this,' Johnstone had said.

Chandler had not written a letter. 'I'll write it when I get back,' he'd quipped.

Having dimmed the cockpit lighting as much as possible, Shilling flew on in the dark.

He again had the lead.

On an airfield south of Bergen, Zürst walked towards his new Bf-110E. For the coming mission, it had everything tagged on: the belly pack, the underwing fuel tanks, the *Schräge Musik*.

'Well, Johann,' he said to Stolberg, 'ready for a long night tour of the fiords?'

'Another quiet night,' Stolberg replied. 'I'm happy with that. This posting is a holiday.'

'I believe in the unforeseen,' Zürst commented. 'Who knows what might happen?'

'Wake me when it's over,' Stolberg said.

They had made every course change at the precise time planned. Though they could not see it, they knew exactly where the Lysander should be. The fact that there was continuing radio silence meant the Lizzie was OK. Any sign of trouble and a sharp bleep would sound on their headphones, as Silverdale alerted them.

Though it had taken off before them, the several changes of course had actually placed it just a mile ahead as they neared the Norwegian coast. When the Lysander made its landing, the Hurricanes would go into a two-minute racetrack pattern that would end just as it would be starting the first leg of the return journey.

If all went as planned.

They'd been airborne now for just over two and a half hours and at the speed they'd been cruising, there was still plenty of fuel left in the drop tanks. Fuel for the return journey was not going to be a problem, even if they were forced to engage in combat.

Shilling glanced over to the left side of the instrument panel where the clock had been specially mounted, just beneath the oxygen regulator. Time soon to begin the racetrack pattern. The Lysander was nearing its landing point.

So far, so good.

Silverdale brought the Lysander low over the myriad skerries of the Norwegian coast, heading for the pre-planned airstrip near Haugesund. He hoped the expected people would be waiting, or Marais would find it hard to explain what a German lieutenant colonel was doing out there at night, all by himself, especially with an active resistance movement on the prowl.

Silverdale's navigation was exact, and he brought the aircraft in to land precisely where it was intended to be, at the precise time. A covering of snow beyond the cleared strip gleamed in the starlight.

The people were waiting.

There was very little conversation. A few soft-spoken snatches. That was all. He was not spoken to. Marais got out and someone else got in. This person too, appeared to be in German uniform. Silverdale was not about to ask about that.

Then, as if by magic, the people and Marais vanished into the gloom beyond the strip and the snow.

Silverdale opened up the throttle and lifted the Lysander off Norwegian soil, banking sharply and pulling into a tight turn to clear some high rocks that he'd been forewarned about. The people who had prepared the strip had sent in exact details of the surrounding terrain. They knew their job.

The Lizzie cleared the snowcapped obstacles and was soon heading low out to sea, on its return journey.

The passenger in the back didn't speak.

Zürst was heading towards Stavanger in his 110. He didn't have much faith in the sensors, which were really at a very early stage of development. He preferred to rely on his own flying skills and his eyesight. It was all right for the scientists to say this or that was the latest thing, but they didn't have to use them. His cannon . . . now that was something he could rely on.

He had brought the Messerschmitt to a low altitude for no particular reason, keeping a good lookout for the ghostly undulations of the unforgiving terrain, to make certain he didn't slam into it.

'I just *saw something*!' Stolberg shouted.

Stolberg had phenomenal eyesight.

Zürst felt a sudden tenseness grip him. 'Are you sure?'

'Positive! It crossed from left to right, just behind us, going west!'

'Call ground control. See if we've got anything up around here.'

Stolberg contacted the controller.

'There are no aircraft authorized in your area,' Zürst heard the controller say. 'Assume it's an enemy.'

'You see, Johann? The unforeseen can happen. What would a Tommy want out here on his own?'

Zürst heaved the 110 round to follow in the direction Stolberg had indicated.

Shilling was instantly alert when the beep sounded on his headphones. The Lysander has spotted something. He immediately jettisoned the tanks and armed the cannon, knowing Chandler would be doing the same.

They then went into a pre-planned series of manoeuvres.

Chandler would position himself at least 2000 feet beneath him, giving a good clearance in the dark, to avoid collision. But the night was such that the aircraft's silhouette could still be seen when close enough, though circumstances would decide at any given time just how much of a margin there would be, in case they came too close during combat.

Meanwhile the Lysander would be hugging the water, making it extremely difficult to spot, heading in a straight line for home at maximum speed while the Hurricanes took on the night-fighter, or night-fighters.

Shilling banked into a wide right-hand turn, describing a circle as he searched out whatever had spooked the Lysander.

Then something huge flashed by, almost on top of him.

'I've seen it again!' Stolberg shouted. 'Going away from us. Turn! Turn!'

Zürst banked the 110 hard, pulling tightly into the turn, and scanning the dark for a sight of the enemy aircraft.

He'd tried using the sensors, but they had proved to be less than encouraging. The scientists needed to do more work.

'He's coming back!' Stolberg was shouting again. 'He's . . .'

The sudden flash of cannon fire lit up the night blindingly. Great blows struck the *Zerstörer*. The entire airframe shook, but there was no explosion. Zürst felt the pungent aroma of spent ammunition clawing at his nostrils.

'That was close!' he said, as he threw the aircraft into a savage turn to the left. The controls seemed to be undamaged.

There was no reply.

'Johann? *Johann! Answer me!*'

A strange gurgling sound responded.

Johann was hit!

Zürst again wheeled the heavy aircraft round, searching out the Tommy who had perhaps killed Stolberg. As he looked up he saw a shape, almost keeping station with him. The underbelly was his. The Tommy clearly didn't know he was there.

He eased forward, positioning the 110 so that the *Schräge Musik* could be brought into play. Without Stolberg to fine-tune his positioning, he'd have to do it by instinct, and *quickly*. This chance would not last long.

One of the modifications on the aircraft of which he definitely approved, was the capability to switch the *Musik* from gunner-operated system to pilot. He now did so swiftly, and fired. The night once more blazed with cannon fire. At that very instant, the Tommy banked away.

Had he scored a hit? Zürst wondered, feeling acute frustration.

The Johann who would have risked his own life to save an enemy pilot or aircrew from the Gestapo, had now been hit – perhaps mortally – by a Tommy. Zürst had once put the question of such a possibility to him.

'We're only doing the same to them,' he'd replied philosophically. 'But they wouldn't torture us if we fell into their hands.'

Even so, Zürst now hoped he had at least struck a blow for Johann.

It was Shilling who had fired at the Messerschmitt. On seeing the vast shape flit by, he had put the Hurricane into another turn, going just wide enough to bring him back to where he'd calculated the enemy aircraft would now be, according to the direction of its movement.

Curving round, he had been gratified to see the well-known shape of the 110 just ahead of and below him, going into a shallow bank, clearly searching for the Hurricane.

He had gone closer in a gentle dive to maintain speed while throttling back to minimize his tell-tale exhausts, and, judging acutely the time when he felt he would be spotted by the gunner, fired.

He'd seen some strikes before the enemy aircraft had lurched violently into a left turn and disappeared.

Then had come a vivid series of flashes over to the right and slightly below.

Had Shippy Chandler scored?

They were still utilizing radio silence, for they had no intention of bringing more unwelcome company racing to the spot. The idea was to end this engagement and get well away before that happened.

Shilling headed for where he'd seen the flashes. Then he suddenly flung the Hurricane on to its back and pulled away just in time, to miss the twin-engined shape that had been coming at him nose on.

Was there more than one Tommy? Zürst now wondered as he once more took violent evasive action as an aircraft nearly slammed into the cockpit.

How else had it got ahead of him? Had he not hit it, after all?

Then he no longer had to worry about that.

A barrage of shells tore into the long cage of the cockpit, exploding within and about it, killing Zürst instantly. The explosions ruptured fuel tanks and the entire aircraft turned into a sunburst that lit up the night.

The careers of Zürst and Stolberg were over.

*　　*　　*

When Shilling had dived away to evade the 110, he'd immediately rolled upright to go into a brief climb, pulled tightly through a loop, rolled upright again, and seen the shape of the Messerschmitt turning to the left below him.

He had curved behind it, matching it in the turn as he drew closer. The gunner was clearly dead, for there had been no sudden movement from the aircraft to indicate that the pilot had been warned of his presence.

Then, when the time was right, he'd fired a two-second burst along the spine and into the cockpit.

It had been enough.

'They'll see that all the way to the North Cape,' Shilling now said briskly on the radio to Chandler. 'Let's head home.'

'With you,' Chandler said.

Something was wrong.

'You OK?'

'I'm fine . . . the Hurri isn't.'

Chandler had been hit. That was what those flashes had been about, Shilling realized.

'Can you make it? We've got to go to radio silence and get out of here as fast as possible.'

'I've got you in sight. I'm hanging on.'

Shilling felt relieved. 'Roger. Call if things get worse.'

'Roger,' Chandler acknowledged.

There was just one more thing Shilling was permitted to do. 'Bright Eyes,' he called. 'Let us know you're OK.'

Immediately, two rapid beeps sounded.

Shilling let out a relieved breath.

'Radio silence. Out.'

They'd been flying close together for over an hour. Soon they'd be back in friendly airspace. They'd heard no alarms from the Lysander, so it was clearly still on course for home.

Shilling felt good. The mission was successful, and they'd got a 110 into the bargain. Miraculously, Chandler wasn't hurt.

Just stay aloft, Shippy, he willed Chandler. Please.

They were well into friendly airspace, but still some distance from home, when Chandler accepted he wasn't going to make it.

'I hate swimming on cold nights,' he murmured calmly as he tried to coax the engine to keep running a little longer.

Remembering Johnstone's warning about the sneak attack from below, he had routinely banked to check the blind spot when streaks of fire had erupted from beneath the aircraft. That unexpected bank had saved him from certain death.

The 110's aim had been ruined, but some shells had still found a target. The Hurricane had rocked with the force of the blows, but had kept on flying as if shaking off the injury as a horse would whisk a fly off its tail.

No vital part of the controls appeared to have been hit and he'd thought he'd escaped reasonably well.

Then the engine gauges had begun to tell a different story. All things considered, he reasoned, the old Hurri had brought him as close to home as it could.

He patted the panel. 'You tried, old girl. Now we must part company. Got to go,' he added briskly to Shilling.

Then the engine began to burp at him. The last breath was coming. It was time to get out.

He sent a Mayday call.

Now get out there!

He remembered the instructor's dry exhortations about leaving a Hurricane safely.

'When abandoning the aircraft, *first* jettison the hood. An important consideration and self-evident, one would think. Not so for some unfortunate, departed souls. Got that, everyone? *Jettison* the hood and *lower your head*, unless you like the idea of being a decapitated chicken. Decrease speed and dive over the side *immediately*. Do *not*, I repeat *do not*, stand on the seat wondering whether your fingernails are dry enough. Delay your exit and you'll modify yourself substantially on either the aerial mast or the tailplane. I hate substantially modified pilots.'

They had laughed nervously and tried not to imagine what bailing out would really be like.

Now *I've* got to do it, Chandler thought.

Remembering everything the instructor had said, he got out cleanly, just as the engine died.

As soon as he'd heard Chandler's emergency call, Shilling sent another Mayday, just to make certain, giving the grid position of Chandler's exit.

Now as he continued to head towards home, he began to worry intensely about his friend down there in the dark, cold waters. Even if he could have circled the spot until help arrived, this was denied him. First priority was to escort the Lysander all the way to a safe landing at Fort Town.

At first light, he decided, he'd go back out there to look for Chandler. He hoped Shippy had got out cleanly.

But for how long would he last in that water,

even with the warm clothing he'd put on for the flight?

And how to tell Susan, if her brother did not survive?

With those thoughts exercising his mind, Shilling shepherded the Lysander safely home.

Johnstone was waiting with the apparently sleepless Creddon and the squadron car. Shilling was driven immediately to the squadron hut, where a hot mug of tea was waiting. Du Toit was there, but there was no sign of either Silverdale or his mystery passenger.

'You won't be seeing them,' Johnstone explained. 'There's an Anson waiting to take them back, and a fresh pilot to ferry the Lysander back at the same time.'

Even as he spoke, the sounds of engines came to them.

'There they go,' Johnstone said.

'That was a mission well executed, Sergeant,' du Toit said. 'Good news on that Me-110. Major Marais' people let us know that their intelligence confirmed the loss of a 110 tonight, in the area where you were active. Sorry about Flying Officer Chandler. I'm certain the Navy are doing everything to find him.'

'I'd like to go up at first light, sir.'

'Quite out of the question. What can you do the Navy can't? Besides, he'll have been in the water for far too long by then.'

'Sir . . .'

'*No*, Sergeant. Now go and get some sleep. Give a full debrief in the morning . . .'

'It's nearly morning now, sir. I could . . .'

'The matter is closed, Sergeant!'

'Sir.'

Johnstone accompanied Shilling to the sergeants' mess.

'I do understand your feelings, young Bob, but on this occasion the CO's right. What can you do?'

'I know where he went down. It's only an hour to first light. I could find him and circle . . .'

'Yes, you could. You could also be court-martialled for disobeying a direct order, whatever your record.'

'Yes, sir.'

The car had stopped.

'Get some sleep. Let's talk later.'

'Yes, sir.'

'And well done. Really well done. I was going to keep it a secret till I was sure, but I believe we may have swung the balance on your commission. I'm looking forward to buying you your first drink as a member of the mess.'

'Thank you, sir. I hope Shippy will be there to drink with us.'

'He will.'

At first light a flurry of snow was falling as Shilling went to his Hurricane. Nobby Clark was there, fussing over it. A fresh swastika had joined the others.

'All fuelled and armed?'

'Yes, Sarge.' Clark pointed to the kills. 'You'll be needing a second row soon.' He had become inordinately proud of working on the aircraft. 'The more the merrier, eh?'

'Indeed, Nobby. I'm off for an air test.'

'Of course, Sarge. Hope you find him.'

Shilling neither confirmed nor denied his intentions. He had no wish to involve anyone in what he was about to do.

He climbed up to the cockpit and got in.

Du Toit was in the mess when he heard the roar of the Merlin. Johnstone was with him.

'What the devil . . . ?' du Toit began furiously.

They both rushed to a window.

'Damn it, young Bob,' Johnstone said softly.

Shilling reached the spot where Chandler had bailed out and began to circle low down over the water, changing the position of the circle every so often.

The light curtain of snow was falling even out there and he peered through his windscreen, searching the water for his close friend.

It seemed very cold down there. If the Navy hadn't found him, Chandler could not possibly have survived. But he didn't want to accept that.

He continued to search.

Three Messerschmitt 109s on a probing mission spotted the circling Hurricane.

They immediately dived to attack.

The Fairey Swordfish seemed to float towards the runway at Fort Town. The biplane fluttered to a landing and taxied to where a pair of Hurricanes were parked.

To everyone's astonishment and joy, Chandler climbed out, safe and well. People were shaking his hand and the Navy pilot's, and patting them vigorously on the back.

But he sensed a sombre mood about them. Nobby Clark was standing before him, looking distraught.

'He went to look for you, sir. Hasn't been back. It's been hours.'

Chandler felt a deep pain in his stomach. He

looked at the faces about him. Then Johnstone was pushing through the crowd. The deputy CO's expression said it all.

'Oh my God,' Chandler cried softly. 'It's . . . it's true?'

Johnstone nodded and took him by the arm, leading him away, while the Navy pilot, looking as grim as the RAF personnel felt, slowly got back into his aircraft.

The Swordfish lifted off as the car took them to the squadron. For once, Creddon had nothing to say.

'The CO ordered him not to go,' Johnstone said. 'I think he felt responsible. He was the leader, you see.' Johnstone cleared his throat noisily.

What am I going to tell Susan? the devastated Chandler thought. What can I possibly say that will console her?

At the squadron, Michaels was waiting for them with some news, but it was not what they'd hoped to hear.

'There was an air battle in grid Baker Four. Two Me-109s went down . . . and one Hurricane. A third 109 was seriously damaged and was seen heading for home. There is some doubt it will make it. They've picked up the bodies of the two German pilots.'

'So Bob's not dead!' Chandler said eagerly. 'He must have bailed out.'

Michaels shook his head slowly. 'There's no sign of him. I'm truly sorry, Shippy.'

Chandler felt his eyes grow hot. 'You know,' he said quietly after a while, 'he didn't bring much with him. There are not many things in his room, I mean. When I clear it out, it will seem as if he's never been here. As if he were invisible.'

Johnstone put a hand on his shoulder. 'He was not invisible to us. He left plenty for us to remember him by.'

At Dispersal, when they heard the news, Nobby Clark said, 'Those kills would have started his second row.' He wiped at his eyes. When he looked up he saw one of the men staring at him.

'Got some dirt in my eye, you pillock!' he growled.

Six weeks later Chandler was on a visit to his home in the Malvern hills. He still vividly remembered the crumpling of Susan's features when he'd been given special leave to go home to tell her the news about Shilling.

Now, as they walked in the grounds, she took his hand in hers and stopped to face him.

'Timmy,' she began in a small voice, 'I'm pregnant.' Then as he stared at her, she went on, 'Why did they take him away from me?' The tears began to pour down her cheeks but, unnervingly, no sobbing came from her. 'You won't let them take my baby away, will you?'

'No one will take your baby away,' he promised firmly. 'That baby is family. *Our* family.' Gently, he wiped at one of the tears. 'Bob, your Jack, did not leave us completely.'

Johnstone was right, Chandler thought. He was not invisible at all.

At Fort Town, du Toit sat at his desk reading a letter that stunned him. It was from Kirsten Willemsteen. The date at the top showed she had written it some time ago. It had been delivered specially from Marais' unit, and did not appear to have been touched by the censors. Marais had died in Norway; his unit did not specify how. Kirsten wrote:

> *I don't know when this will get to you. I've given this to Hennie Marais to deliver, but it will depend on when he finds you. Hennie has told me why you no longer showed any interest in me. He did a terrible thing and I believe this is his way of atoning. Did you*

really think so little of me to believe that your family history would stop me loving you? I have never stopped loving you. I have not married . . .

Du Toit felt his eyes filming over and stopped reading for the time being. He thought of all the bitterness that had lived within him, and of the things it had made him do. He thought of the pain he had caused Kirsten, and of what he had done to Shilling.

'Dear God,' he said softly. 'Forgive me.'

Outside, a pair of Hurricanes took off on patrol.

TITLES IN SERIES FROM 22 BOOKS

Available now at newsagents and booksellers or use the order form provided

continued overleaf . . .

All at £4.99

All 22 Books are available at your bookshop, or can be ordered from:

22 Books
Mail Order Department
Little, Brown and Company
Brettenham House
Lancaster Place
London WC2E 7EN

Alternatively, you may fax your order to the above address. Fax number: 0171 911 8100.

Payments can be made by cheque or postal order, payable to Little, Brown and Company (UK), or by credit card (Visa/Access). Do not send cash or currency. UK, BFPO and Eire customers, please allow 75p per item for postage and packing, to a maximum of £7.50. Overseas customers, please allow £1 per item.

While every effort is made to keep prices low, it is sometimes necessary to increase cover prices at short notice. 22 Books reserves the right to show new retail prices on covers which may differ from those previously advertised in the books or elsewhere.

NAME ....

ADDRESS ....

....

....

☐ I enclose my remittance for £_____
☐ I wish to pay by Access/Visa

Card number
☐☐☐☐ ☐☐☐☐ ☐☐☐☐ ☐☐☐☐

Card expiry date
☐☐ ☐☐

Please allow 28 days for delivery. Please tick box if you do not wish to receive any additional information ☐